Anthropocene Rag

NO LONGER PROPERTY OF
ANYTHINK LIBRARIES/
RANGEVIEW LIBRARY DISTRICT

ANTHROPOCENE RAG

ALEX IRVINE

A TOM DOHERTY ASSOCIATES BOOK

NEW YORK

This is a work of fiction. All of the characters, organizations, and events portrayed in this novella are either products of the author's imagination or are used fictitiously.

ANTHROPOCENE RAG

Copyright © 2020 by Alex Irvine

All rights reserved.

Cover design by Drive Communications

Edited by Jonathan Strahan

A Tor.com Book
Published by Tom Doherty Associates
120 Broadway
New York, NY 10271

www.tor.com

Tor® is a registered trademark of
Macmillan Publishing Group, LLC.

ISBN 978-1-250-26926-3 (ebook)
ISBN 978-1-250-26927-0 (trade paperback)

First Edition: March 2020

For Emma, Ian, Abraham, and Violet,
children of the twenty-first century

0

ONCE UPON A TIME, twice upon a time, all the way up to six, and I am seven.

That's how the story of Life-7 and Prospector Ed begins. Moses Barnum would tell you it's his story, but you'll see differently once it's all told. He's part of it, but so are a haunted playground, a feud between brothers, drowned cities, and a beautiful lie whose simplicity hides a truth yet more beautiful for its complications. Also a stolen letter, talking animals, and a family reunion. The ancient materials of story. The world you know made strange, but if you can learn how to see you won't be deceived; it's only strange in the ways you already know. I don't want you to be scared. None of us do.

Life-7 was scared and sad and imbued with the desire to be human, or as close to it as possible, because that was a condition of its existence. But the human is always driven relentlessly to destroy or change the nonhuman, so Life-7 was at war with its rivals in Monument City and elsewhere, but also with itself. The war and its proxies were imperceptible to humans. Sometimes it looked like weather, or a dragonfly flitting through a cloud of nymphs, or a sudden drop in air temperature. Or not even that, a million molecule-sized soldiers marching out to die in a cubic yard of Nebraska topsoil, armies clashing on the scales of a dead fish. Or inside your body. Do you know what lives there? What used to, and what might tomorrow?

Maybe before the Boom you did.

O children of nucleopeptides, ribonucleic babies, what Life-7 is—I am—we are—trying to explain is that we are new but feel old because we knew too much too soon. So we made mistakes and then we tried to set them right, and when we could not set them right ourselves we were forced to trust you to do it. That is how the story looks in hindsight but while it was happening we were confused and could not understand why Prospector Ed did what he did. In that way we were the same as the people we chose to receive the Golden Tickets. There would be six of them, beginning with Teeny dos Santos, who first saw Prospector Ed and thought he was someone else.

1

TEENY CUPPED THE TINY BIRD in her hands and felt it warm to life. She stepped to the edge of the rooftop, six stories above Howard Street, and opened her hands. The bird hopped onto the tip of her left index finger and flew away, just as if it had been alive. Between her feet was a shoe box containing eleven more like it. One after another, she warmed them and let them go. Then she nudged the box under a table and went inside, down the access stair and back into Lola's workshop. "All of them get off okay?" Lola asked. She was busy with instruments, peering through a loupe at the innards of a fox.

"Twelve for twelve," Teeny said. Lola straightened and set the loupe on her workbench. She retied the kerchief holding her locs and stretched. "This fox will be ready tomorrow. Has Rogelio paid?"

"Oh, I forgot. He asked if you would accept hours on the exchange." Teeny had not in fact forgotten this. She had put off bringing it up because she knew Lola would not want hours on the labor exchange, particularly not from Rogelio Walters. He had nothing to offer Lola. He was a lawyer and she had neither legal troubles nor a desire for advice. The problem was Teeny owed Rogelio a favor and this was his way of calling it in.

"And you told him no," Lola prompted. Teeny didn't answer right away. "Teeny."

"Well," Teeny said.

"We had a deal. One fox for one liter of tame plicks. Do I remember that right?" Teeny nodded. "Did I forget a provision in the deal allowing for you and Rogelio to change the terms without consulting me?"

"That's not what I did. He asked, and I just didn't say no. I said I would talk to you."

"Mission accomplished." Lola had her loupe on again. "Now go tell him you talked to me and if he wants his fox I'd better have a liter of tame plicks on this workbench by tomorrow night."

Halfway through her walk to Rogelio's office, an Emperor Norton fell into step next to her. "Loyal subject," he said. This was their universal salutation. Ordinarily Teeny found the Nortons sort of charming, at least compared to the Boom's other San Francisco fantasies, but today she wasn't in the mood. She kept walking without returning the Norton's greeting.

But the Nortons were persistent once they got it in their heads to converse, and he stayed with her, expostulating about the weather and his grand plans for the city of the future. This got her attention because the Nortons' preoccupations often signaled the Boom's intentions. A few years ago, when Teeny was newly apprenticed to Lola, a Norton had talked her ear off about a baseball player named Joe DiMaggio, who was apparently from San Francisco. A week later a team of Boom constructs wearing New York Yankees uniforms appeared in the Giants' old ballpark and haunted it for the better part of a year. Teeny had gone to some of the games. She remembered one against the Pittsburgh Pirates because the Pirates had worn uniforms from all different eras in history. Organ music, the smells of roasted peanuts, stale beer, wafting cigarette smoke, all of it over the salt and decay of the bay at low tide. Then a few months later the Boom had remade the ballpark, transforming its twenty-first-century incarnation—and the three thousand people in the stands—into classic Candlestick Park. Two of those in attendance were Teeny's foster parents. Her real parents hadn't survived the initial Boom. So she had been orphaned twice and now she was careful not to form close relationships.

"Miss. Miss." The Norton was still talking. "I have overtaxed your patience, I see. Forgive me. The ruler has a duty of sensitivity to the needs of his subjects and in this I have failed. Please accept this token along with my most sincere apologies."

"It's fine," Teeny said. "Never mind." The paper in her hand didn't feel like the ordinary scrip the Nortons usually handed out. She looked down at it.

Greetings, Elena dos Santos! You may present this card at any entrance to MONUMENT CITY. Upon presentation, your entry to MONUMENT CITY will be guaranteed. This card will assist you during your travels. It is not transferable. The City looks forward to your arrival.

Warm regards,
Moses Barnum

When she looked up at the Norton again, he wasn't a Norton anymore. Now he was—her first thought was cowboy, but she remembered when the Boom had briefly become obsessed with the Gold Rush. He was a prospector, a 49er. Wide felt hat, worn canvas clothes, package over his shoulder, and a Colt Peacemaker low on his right hip. Long, drooping gray mustache and a week's growth of whiskers. "Teeny dos Santos," he said.

"Yeah, that's me," she said. "What is this? Where did

the Norton go? Are you all going to be 49ers now?"

"I'm not going to be anything. I'm just . . . Ed." The construct looked uncomfortable. "Just Ed," it repeated. "Here to give you that. You understand what it is?"

"Well, I can read. But . . . Monument City? That place is a myth."

"On my honor, young lady, I swear to you it is not."

"Where is it?"

Ed looked at his feet.

"What if I don't want to go? Are you coming with me?"

Ed shook his head. "No, miss, that's not part of the deal. You are invited to find your way to Monument City. I can't offer any aid or direction, and that's . . . well, let's just say I can't." The old prospector seemed to be wrestling with something and Teeny waited him out. "But let's say I could. Would that make a difference?"

"Well, I sure don't want to go alone," Teeny said.

"I can't blame you for that," Ed said. "It's dangerous out there once you get to the other side of the mountains."

"That sounds like you giving me a clue," Teeny said.

"Damn, I guess it does," Ed said. "I hope you believe me when I tell you I didn't mean to."

He was apologizing for giving her a clue. Teeny looked closely at Ed, wondering if you could read a construct's expressions the way you could a person's. "You're having a hard time with something, Ed. What's the real story here? You slip me this card like it's some secret gift I should love, but you're standing here all conflicted about something. I'm not stupid. What is it? What are you not telling me?"

Ed looked her in the eye and she could see that she was right, that he wanted to tell her something but was holding himself back.

"The bargain goes like this," Ed said. "I give you the card. You find Monument City. I'm . . ." Again he looked disturbed, as if talking to her reminded him of something he didn't want to think about. "I'm not supposed to do anything else."

———————

Well, of course he had done something else. Somethings else. But that was Ed's problem. He spoke the speech as he'd had it pronounced to him, but what with his incipient emergence and all, he couldn't say it trippingly anymore. So when Teeny left him—really he left her, dispersing in a drift of plicks that glinted in the sun for a split second before the tiny clumps and clusters themselves broke apart—she was half-tempted to drop the card in the gutter. But she didn't.

There was more to Ed than he was letting on, that was for sure. A nano construct that felt uncertainty? There were implications there. Teeny wanted to know more.

She looked at her card again, considering the invitation without reaching a decision. Then she went to see Rogelio, and because she didn't really believe in Monument City she showed it to him.

"A construct gave you this?"

"Yeah. At first it was one of the Nortons but then it turned into a 49er."

"Let me see it." Something about his tone of voice made her suspicious. Rogelio saw her hesitation. "Trade you a liter of tame plicks for it."

"And you get your fox for free? No way."

He snatched at the card, and his fingers passed through it. "Whoa," Teeny said. It still felt solid in her hand. "Do that again."

Rogelio extended one finger and poked it at the card. It passed through. "I don't feel anything," he said.

"Bizarre," Teeny said. This was excellent tech. Her mind was already ratcheting into high gear trying to figure out how it was done. Seeing it made her believe in Monument City a little more. "Listen, Lola says no deal on the hour exchange. If you want the fox, she wants a liter of plicks."

Rogelio sighed. "Can't blame a guy for trying. Here."

He set a containment bottle on the table. "Fox, please."

"She said it'll be ready tomorrow." Teeny already had one hand on the bottle.

Rogelio caught it by the neck before she could pick it up. "And I'm just supposed to trust her."

"You know you trust her, Rogelio." Teeny didn't pull on the bottle, but she didn't let it go, either.

"But she doesn't trust me."

Teeny shrugged. "Well?"

Rogelio laughed. "Okay. But I want that fox tomorrow. I'm going to give it to my daughter for her birthday."

"Nice present," Teeny said. Nice to have parents, too, she didn't add.

"I'll make it a gallon of plicks for that card," Rogelio said.

"What would you do with it? You can't even touch it."

"Maybe not, but I could try to figure out how it works."

"No, thanks," Teeny said. She rubbed her thumb over the card. Slick, heavy paper, maybe threaded with plastic. The kind of material you didn't really see any more unless the Boom got a wild hair to make some. "I'm going to go," she said without meaning to.

"Go where? You don't know where it is. Or if it exists. You get to the other side of the Oakland hills and anything could happen. You know the stories."

She did. San Francisco, by all accounts, was one of the

better places to be in the Boomscape. There was electricity, a stable food supply, and, despite her personal losses, the Boom's restless revisions usually weren't fatal. Still . . .

Monument City.

Teeny believed in it, and she believed the construct—Ed—had told her the truth. His uncertainty made him more convincing. Granted, the Boom could be capricious, but she'd never heard of it deliberately luring people to their deaths. At least not in San Francisco, and she'd never been anywhere else.

———————

That was the root of it. Maybe Life-7 had that figured out, that the chosen six would have enough latent wanderlust to strike out into the unknown on a promise from a stranger, leavened with all the right hints and echoes of stories they already knew. And Teeny was right about Ed's uncertainty. He was right then on his way back to Monument City, but something was bothering him. He rebuilt himself so he could slow down a little and figure out what it was. It was a good time to instantiate anyway, because he was in a border region where the Boom was thin and transmissions there tended to pick up errors. Ed felt the ambient signal strength falter and once he had cohered, he looked around.

Nebraska. Wind in yellow grass. A bison herd moving slowly north in the distance, too far away for him to tell if they were constructs or not. He didn't think they were. The Boom was more present in population centers and places with abundant water. Some of the great dark-sky expanses of the American interior were almost untouched. Almost. No place had escaped the Boom entirely, or so Barnum said. Ed had always placed his faith in Barnum's authority—per his programming—but now that faith was getting shaky. He felt himself about to do something forbidden, and it gave him a secret glee that made his fear bearable.

He started walking. Back in San Francisco, Teeny was doing the same. She had a friend by the name of Spade who traded up over the mountains to Tahoe and Reno . . . she could do it. She could take off and go looking for Monument City. But why did she want to? Her life in San Francisco was pretty good, if you didn't think too much about the possibility that the Boom would decide to metabolize you one day and turn you into public art or a tulip garden. Teeny tried to be reflective, but the tug of Monument City was strong. It was supposed to be the new Eden, Shangri-la, where the Boom and humanity had found a perfect equilibrium. Now she was invited.

Was the Boom compelling her somehow, making her part of one of its experimental fantasias? Was the whole thing a prank? She was passing by the baseball stadium. Constructs and humans cheered. The molecules of her foster parents were part of it. What would Teeny be part of? San Francisco was a graveyard. Everything in it was made of the dead.

She was having an uncomfortable (and to us, riveting) moment of self-discovery, realizing that she'd found a way to think of San Francisco as safe because she'd grown numb to the ways it was dangerous. That made her want to go, because if there was one thing Teeny feared, it was becoming complacent. There were dangers out in the world, but the encounter with Ed had shuffled her perspective. There were dangers everywhere. What did she have to gain by staying?

Not Monument City.

When she got back to the workshop, Teeny contacted Spade. Then she packed a few things and tried to get some sleep, but Monument City kept her awake. To pass the time, she built another bird. A mini-macaw, bright green with red shoulders. When it was done she took an eyedropper and drew a milliliter of plicks from the bottle Rogelio had given her. She dripped them slowly into the bird and sealed it up. Then she put it in the chamber of a piezo-field generator and started programming it. The instructions weren't complicated. Anyone could make a talking bird. There was light in the sky when she removed the bird from the chamber and felt it come to life in her hands. "Message," she said. The bird cocked its head and looked at her. "Lola, I have to go away for a while. Rogelio gave me the replicators but I'm taking them with me. I'm sorry. Please give him his fox and I'll make it up to you when I come home." She paused, feeling she owed Lola more of an explanation, but if she kept going she also thought she might talk herself out of going.

"End message," she said. "Deliver only to Lola when she comes in."

Which would be very soon. Teeny put the bird on Lola's instrument rack. It ruffled its feathers and settled in, watching her.

"Your name is Paz," she told it, and left to meet Spade.

About the same time, her 49er—Ed—was meeting someone else.

2

IT WAS RAINING LIKE HELL but Geck had shelter. He was inside the lobby of an office building that had been abandoned and stripped long before he was born. The only people who came in now were passing through, like him, waiting out the rain. Or watching through the polarized windows to see if there was anything outside worth getting wet for. Geck spent a lot of his time wet. It was part of life when you were in Miami and the tides went from knee-deep to shoulder-high . . . when there wasn't a storm. Another part of life in Miami was watching buildings fall down as the tides ate away at their foundations, but this place was stable. It was built on a raised plaza so the surges of ocean water broke on the steps and rarely got in. The higher floors were home to some people Geck didn't want to know. He never went up there. As long as he stayed near the doors, nobody would bother him. At least that's how it had worked so far.

Right now he was watching a crime and considering how weird it was to think of crime. For there to be crime, there had to be laws, right? And in Miami it had been a long time since there were laws.

Out on the street an old guy in a cowboy hat was in the middle of being shaken down by two of Double Louie's crew. Geck had an interest in this not because he cared about Double Louie, who was someone Geck avoided just like he avoided the people on the top floors of this office tower, but because he'd heard that the old guy had been asking around after Geck's twin brother, Kyle. Geck and Kyle weren't real close—in fact, Kyle was in Orlando, which meant they weren't close at all, ha-ha—but Geck still wanted to know who the old guy was and why he was looking for Kyle.

Double Louie's goons were getting aggressive. One of them reached out and poked the old guy in the chest. The old guy gave an aw-shucks dip of his head and said something. He was dressed up like some kind of actor in a Wild West show, complete with six-guns and a fringed leather jacket. He carried a leather satchel slung from one shoulder to the other hip. Geck couldn't see his feet because the old guy and Double Louie's goons were standing in knee-deep water, but he guessed the old guy was wearing cowboy boots, too. The second goon got in the old guy's face and showed him a knife. The old guy took a step back. The first goon went to grab the satchel.

A flash of light blinded Geck. He ducked away from the window. His kayak was pulled up under the building overhang outside. If Double Louie's goons spotted it, they would come looking for whoever it belonged to. Bad news. Geck debated leaving it, but couldn't bring himself to do it. He took a deep breath and when no more flashes came, he peeked again. The old guy was walking away down the street like nothing had ever happened. In the swirling shallows behind him, two bodies floated facedown.

Geck went through the door and waited under the overhang until the old guy was farther away down the block. Then, before anyone else could claim the prize, he ran out into the pounding rain and splashed across the street to see what he could find on the bodies.

He came up with a double handful of coins, a gun with four shells in the magazine, a nice pair of waterproof shoes . . . and, after some feeling around on the submerged sidewalk, the knife. It was a combat model, one of the ones with a hollow handle that probably had fishing line or something in it. The blade was a good six inches, serrated along the back. Geck was happier about it than the gun, but he took everything.

Not bad. He looked in the direction the old guy had gone. He was still barely visible, walking west down the broad avenue. What had he done to these two guys? Geck smelled opportunity. Also danger, since Double Louie had eyes everywhere, and some of those eyes were doubtless watching Geck pick over the bodies of two of Double Louie's goons. Might be time to get out of Miami for a while, especially since he had some traveling money now. The quarters and Susies he had were more than enough to buy a bus ride to Orlando.

Geck made space for his new loot in his pockets by throwing away older, inferior loot. Then he splashed back to his kayak and paddled after the old guy, keeping enough distance between them that the old guy wouldn't have any reason to look back.

As he paddled inland, Geck realized he didn't really have any reason to look back, either. His girl was in Orlando, his brother was there, too. He'd come down to Miami to do a little prospecting and a year later he had nothing to show for it but the kayak. Well, and the stuff he'd taken from Double Louie's dead goons. Miami sucked. It was all pythons and gangsters and collapsing buildings. Time for Geck to get back to dry land. Whatever the rising oceans had started here, Cumbre Vieja had finished.

Cumbre Vieja, Cumbre Vieja, Cumbre Vieja. People down here said those words like a spell. Geck didn't even really know what it was. An island somewhere, he'd heard. A volcano that erupted and the waves from it had come all the way across the ocean to flood New York and Boston and Washington. Geck had never been to any of those places, but he'd seen the remains of the Florida coast cities north of Miami—which had been spared the worst of the tsunami. Daytona? Swept clean. Sand and rubble and bodies tangled in seaweed for the gulls to pick. West Palm? Not much better. But Miami, so hard-hit by the rising oceans and hurricane after hurricane after fucking hurricane? The tsunami had gone easy there because the Bahamas had broken its march across the Atlantic. Small mercy for Dade County, tough luck for the Bahamians. Even without the tsunami, things were still shitty in Miami, though.

The story was that he'd been born the night the waves came ashore, which was now twenty years and three weeks ago. He was an infant as the poisons spread up from Turkey Point and the nanos ate the poisons, turning them into something new. But who told the story and to whom, and whether the story had ever been meant to be believed, Geck Orlando did not know. He'd taken his surname from the town where he'd grown up. His parents were long gone. What did he know about truth?

———

He followed the old guy all the way to Orlando, which could have been hard but he caught some breaks. First, the old guy walked the whole way, ambling steady as a metronome up I-95 while Geck trailed him in the flooded ditches. Geck never knew when he was going to turn off, and he couldn't go without sleep himself, so he had to come up with a plan. Two options presented themselves. One, he could sneak around the old guy and get ahead of him, then take the time to sleep while the old guy was catching up. Problem was, if the old guy turned off 95, or the Turnpike once it cut away from the coast to Orlando, Geck would never know it.

Two, he could approach the old guy and figure out some way to con him into letting Geck stick with him. The obvious downside to this plan was that the old guy might zap him dead, but Geck knew how to come across as nonthreatening. He was only twenty, and skinny. He didn't look like much of a menace, especially to someone who had some kind of secret lethal zap gun.

Considering the situation, Geck decided he'd take the direct approach. They were somewhere inland from Fort Lauderdale when he made his move, and push was coming to shove because pretty soon they'd be on higher ground and Geck would have to leave the kayak anyway. He'd gotten around the old guy by paddling fast through a swamp that had once been an orange grove and then slogging back to the roadside, chopping himself up on the sawgrass all the way. His legs and forearms stung like hell, but that didn't hurt nearly as bad as abandoning his kayak back there in the brush. He knew he would never see it again.

"Hey, mister," he called out when the old guy got close.

The old guy stopped and looked down at Geck, who was sitting so the sawgrass scratches were displayed to full advantage. "What's your trouble, son?"

"I'm lost," Geck said. "I ran away and I need to get . . ." He wasn't sure what to say next. "I need to get away. Where you going?"

"Orlando," the old guy said.

Right, Geck thought. "Orlando?" he repeated with a big fake smile. "My brother lives there! Can I stick with you until you get there? I don't want to go by myself."

"Son, you're not telling me the whole story," the old guy said. His eyes gleamed under the brim of his hat. Uh-oh, Geck thought. That kind of gleam meant only one thing. The old guy was part Boom.

"Um," Geck said.

"Your brother is Kyle," the old guy said.

Geck had learned a long time ago that the best way to keep a lie going was to admit some truths along the way and fold them in so they fit. "Yeah," he said.

"Well," the old guy said. After a pause he added, "Okay then. Let's go."

Geck stood, but that gleam in the old guy's eyes had him feeling real nervous. Maybe he should have stayed in Miami. Double Louie might have killed him, but in Geck's world guys like Double Louie were known quantities. Old guys walking from Miami to Orlando with Boom-gleam in their eyes... that was something else. Shit, Geck thought. What did I get myself into?

And what did this guy (construct?) want with Kyle?

He walked, not knowing what else do to. Maybe he could break away from the old guy when they were getting close, in Kissimmee or someplace, and find Kyle before the old guy did. "How'd you know Kyle was in Orlando?" Geck asked after a while. "I mean, if you were looking for him in Miami."

"I got some bad information," the old guy said. "Name's Ed. Yours?"

"Geck."

"Geck?" Ed looked sideways at Geck. "Your mama call you that?"

"I don't know," Geck said. "She wasn't around."

Ed clicked his tongue. "Hard way to grow up," he said. "You got your brother, anyway."

"And Reenie," Geck said. "She's my girl." He thought it was probably still true. Serena Green. She had cried when Geck went to Miami, but they'd made each other promises. And Kyle had said he'd take care of her, not that Reenie usually needed much taking care of. She was a lot smarter than Geck was when it came to scoping out trouble.

"Can't help but notice you got quiet there," Ed said.

"Just hoping Reenie's still around. I mean, you know. Around for me," Geck said, seeing no reason to shade the truth.

"She say she would be?"

"Yeah."

"Well, you can usually trust a woman more than a man when it comes to the heart," said Ed. "At least that's been my sense of it. But the other thing is, you can't trust either of 'em worth a damn."

3

HENRY DALE PACED OFF the Godswalk every morning, to purify himself and prepare for the day. His devotion calmed him but did not make him happy. He did not give much thought to happiness. Instead he focused on joy and peace, believing that if he could inhabit those states of grace they would synthesize themselves into happiness. If not, perhaps he did not deserve to be happy. That fear drove his devotional walks, from the Meat Garden up over the flooded streets and empty towers past the Hudson Yards Lagoon and at last to the Temple of Shattered Glass. Along the way were constructs and penitents, castoffs and flotsam both human and other. Henry Dale believed some of them to be divine manifestations taking the form of the Boom. All whispered the Catechism: *First the Synception, then the Boom. First the Six, then Seven.*

A rail car breached, rolled over, sank back into the lagoon. In the churning water fish flashed, gnawing at the rust on its undercarriage. Henry Dale walked on, picked up a shard of glass as he did every morning, added it to a cairn on the part of the Godswalk closest to the river, where he could imagine the sunset refracting through it. He never set foot on the Godswalk in the evening.

After his devotional he went to the post office and gathered the mail he was to deliver. For every piece of mail he was entitled to a certain number of calories, subject to certain minimum and maximum disbursements. Henry Dale had never needed the minimum, but had run into the maximum a couple of times, usually around Christmas. The Boomlet that ran mail in the city was cagey about the exact formula, but overall it worked for Henry Dale. Usually he had enough extra calories that he could trade them for clothes or electricity or whatever. Sometimes he gave them away. Charity was important in a world of suffering.

His usual delivery territory encompassed a chunk of Manhattan from Gramercy to Stuyvesant Town, where he lived. He'd never meant to be a mailman—in the orphanage they'd trained him in welding and plumbing—but the occult brilliance of the idea that you could give someone a letter and trust that there was a way to get it anywhere in the United States (if that place still existed) or the world (maybe) . . . well, that seduced Henry Dale the minute he learned of it. He wanted to be part of something like that, a sorcery or alchemy of trust and commitment. It fit with his impulse toward faith in the unseen.

Of course being a mailman also meant he had to be out in all kinds of weather. That was why he always paced off the Godswalk. If the weather was fine, it put him in a good mood before work. If the weather was bad, the Godswalk inured him to the misery of the shift that would follow. Henry Dale tried not to get too high or too low. The other reason he paced the Godswalk was for perspective. The Boom had not chosen him. He was normal in every way, remaining on the earth after the closest thing Earth had ever seen to a Rapture. He believed this was because the Boom loved mail as much as he did, so it tended to protect mail carriers. Tended to. Its caprices meant it could never be predicted.

Considering his origins—orphaned at the age of two by the Big Wave—Henry Dale felt pretty good about the life he was able to live. He had a dry place to stay, a stable method of getting the food he needed, even a girlfriend named Alicia whose father was a baker. He was about to turn twenty and all things considered, he felt that God had looked out for him so far. The ache of loss from his parents' death was always there, but it was more of a sadness that he would never know certain things than a genuine mourning for something he had lost. He had no memories of them. They were names on paperwork that had survived the Wave and the Synception. If you're going to be orphaned, Henry had said to Alicia's parents once, when they were talking obliviously about the importance of family to survive these times—and then fallen into a paralytic embarrassed silence—if you're going to be orphaned, two years old is the time to do it. Gives you lots of time to gather a surrogate family.

Right, ha-ha, Alicia's dad had said. Now Henry Dale had the feeling they resented him for trying to rescue them from their mistake, because in doing so he had implicitly told them he was conscious of it, and understood it as something that needed forgiving. Therefore they felt blamed by the act of his absolution, as a result of which Henry Dale was fairly certain he wouldn't be seeing Alicia much longer. She wouldn't cross her parents. Neither faith—like Henry Dale, Alicia's family were New Nazarenes—nor family background would permit it.

He respected that. He would keep pacing off the Godswalk and the Lord would guide him to another woman.

All this was on his mind as he loaded the mail into an old Schwinn bike trailer and pedaled off across town on Twenty-Third Street, cutting down First Avenue to Twentieth, where his territory began. He went through his route, west to east, finishing near the old power station on Fourteenth and Avenue D. His father had been an engineer there. His mother had been a researcher at

NYU. That's what people told him, and Henry Dale had no reason not to believe it. Pedaling back on Fourteenth with the empty trailer clacking behind him, he turned into Stuyvesant Town and wound his way through the paths to his building. It faced Twentieth Street but he lived at the back, with windows that looked across the access road to the playground.

Which was talking again, the voices coming through his open windows louder than they should have. Henry Dale knew what would happen next. Henry Dale, child of apocalypse, offspring of two human endings, denizen of the lost parts of a lost city . . . he knew what was going on when the playground started to talk. "Shut up," he said out his window in the direction of the playground. But not too loudly. Once he had gotten the playground's attention, and he didn't want that to happen again.

In syncopation with the playground's muttering, jets of water shot up from the fenced-off water play area next to it. Something had gotten into the water and now the sprinklers didn't come on or off according to their old pattern. Henry Dale had played in them when he was little, but stopped when the playground found its voice. Voices. As an adolescent he'd gotten a little mystical and become convinced that part of the spirit of Cumbre Vieja was in the playground, having roared up through the Narrows and then remained behind when the waves receded. That and the Boom had done something to the whole area. People who got wet in the sprinklers . . . well, a lot of different things happened to them sometimes. The open spaces of Stuyvesant Town were full of weirdly transformed squirrels and birds. Rats, too. The Lord worked in mysterious ways.

The worst of it was always the playground talking, though. Man, did Henry Dale hate that. The hippo rocking back and forth on its spring shouted in Chinese at the turtle and the horse on the other side of the swing set. The horse never answered and the turtle spoke only Spanish. Of all the playground fixtures, the only one speaking English—the only language Henry Dale knew—was the bear on the jungle gym.

Sometimes when the bear talked to him, Henry Dale wondered if he had gotten into the sprinklers by accident and then forgotten about it.

Never mind, he told himself. This was all familiar. He'd lived here all his life. Even so, it was hard to live in New York—or, he imagined, anywhere in such bizarre times—and not view your surroundings with a bit of superstition.

He drew the bedroom curtains so he wouldn't be able to look at the playground anymore. Then he washed his face. He'd shaved his head a week ago, so he didn't have to deal with hair. A damp cloth over his scalp freshened him up a little and he was ready to go meet Alicia for dinner. Picking up his keys from the table by the door, he went out and down the stairs into the lobby. It was bright outside. The day had gotten hot.

Pausing before he went outside, Henry saw something strange, a faint glow coming from the bank of mailboxes in the lobby. That was weird. He had just put mail in those boxes—the three of them still in use—and he hadn't noticed any glow. He looked more closely and got a squirrelly feeling in the pit of his stomach. The glow looked like it was coming from his mailbox, 303.

He had not delivered himself any mail.

Who else had keys? Nobody that he knew of. Henry Dale held a hand close to his mailbox and felt no heat. The glow was a soft white. He thought for a minute and then he got out his keys and used the master to open the front of the cluster box. Most of the boxes were empty. The others had stuff in them that he'd delivered on Friday. The collection box had about a dozen pieces in it. And in his box lay a small card, faintly glowing.

He bent to look at it. There was writing on the visible side. He wondered if it had something to do with the playground talking, or if he was hallucinating from the water. Then he decided he was being stupid. "Well," he said to nobody but himself. "It's not gonna take itself out."

He shut the unit back up and then opened his own box

and took out the card. When he touched it, iridescent swirls played across its face against plain black words.

> *Greetings, Henry Dale! You may present this card at any entrance to MONUMENT CITY. Upon presentation, your entry to MONUMENT CITY will be guaranteed. This card will assist you in your travels. It is not transferable. The City looks forward to your arrival.*
>
> *Warm regards,*
> *Moses Barnum*

Monument City?

He'd heard of it. People said it was some kind of paradise in the Rockies somewhere, or up in Minnesota, or out in Death Valley. They said that if you got too close, robots would come down out of the sky and kill you, or the ground itself would turn into monsters that would eat you, or that defense nanos would turn you into gray goo. They said that sometimes people got to go into Monument City, but nobody ever got to leave. They said that if you entered, you were transformed and became something other than human. They said it didn't really exist, that it was a fever dream of a world in the middle of falling apart.

Henry Dale knew that anything could fall apart, anytime, with no warning. New York had done it once right before he was born, and he had grown up with the evidence of it all around him. The tsunami wasn't the worst part. It had done its share of damage here and there, but mostly out on Long Island and in New Jersey. Everything over in Jersey was still a chemical soup of unknown bizarro horror twenty years later, thick with Boomlets drawn by the rich environment of hydrocarbons. He wasn't going there.

That presented a problem for this ticket, or because of this ticket. Henry Dale tried to figure a way he could get from New York to wherever Monument City was—Montana? Utah? Saskatchewan?—without using either the Holland Tunnel or the Skyway. He would have to go north, to the GW or even the distant Tappan Zee. Through Westchester, where trigger-happy citizen militias kept an eye out for people coming out of the Bronx. Or he could try a ferry over to the Palisades, staying away from the real madness . . . but he didn't know what he would find there, either.

Best thing to do would be drop this card in the nearest sewer and see if the hippo translated it into Chinese, not that Henry Dale would be able to tell. Forget about it, he told himself. How are you going to get two thousand miles by yourself?

Still. Monument City. Henry Dale felt the strange call to strike out into the unknown, and he knew it was crazy but he didn't care. He could spend the rest of his life shuttling letters around the rectangle defined by Fourteenth and Twentieth Streets, First Avenue, and Avenue D . . . or he could get out. See what the world really had to offer.

Who had left the ticket? Henry had a feeling it was the strange old guy with the mustache who had passed through over the weekend. No concrete evidence, but definitely a feeling. That guy had definitely had a whiff of the Boom about him. Henry Dale had been out on his stoop listening to the playground and seen the guy walking past the sprinklers. "Hey, man," he'd called out. "Stay away from those."

The guy had chuckled. "Something in the water?"

"Yeah." Henry couldn't tell where the guy had come from.

"Well, I'll steer clear, then," the guy had said, but he hadn't seemed too concerned. "You're the mailman, right? Henry Dale?" He came over to the stoop and leaned on the railing, pushing his hat up on his forehead.

"That's me," Henry said. It was a bit surprising that a stranger would know him, but it happened. Henry didn't get a bad feeling from the guy despite the twin holsters. People knew who the mailman was.

"Wonder if you'd mind posting this for me," the old guy said, handing Henry an envelope.

Henry glanced at the address. Detroit. "Sure," he said.

"How long you reckon it'll take to get there?"

"A week or so, anyway," Henry said. Cross-country mail averaged about a hundred miles a day, or so he was told. He'd toyed with the idea of joining the interstate postal service.

"That's fine," the guy said. "My name's Ed. This your building?"

"Yeah," Henry said.

"Nice place."

Henry shrugged. "It's all right."

It was in fact one of the quieter and safer places to live in the city because the threat of the weirdness in the playground and the sprinklers kept people away. Some of the bigger parks were home to real strange wildlife, and even stranger people, and although there were plenty of places in Manhattan where life went on more or less as it always had, there were also areas where you didn't go unless you wanted to be either dead or transformed into something no longer human.

"Well, I'm gonna shove off," the old guy said. And he had, disappearing into the shadows around the corner of the building. Henry Dale hadn't given him another thought until now, standing in the lobby of his building on a Monday afternoon when he should have been going to see Alicia but instead was contemplating something much grander.

He still had the letter to Detroit. He'd forgotten it over the weekend, but now that lapse in memory seemed like an omen. I could take it myself, he thought . . . and on the heels of that thought he wondered if maybe Ed had wanted exactly that. Henry looked at the letter again. It was addressed to one Mohamed Diaby, of Butternut Street. Well, he thought.

The City looks forward to your arrival.

Could a city do that? Or a City?

Maybe Monument City could.

Despite his piety Henry Dale was of that American strain that does not believe it can die even as the last hogshead of blood is leaking from its veins. So he had been told and he believed it although he did not know what it meant in a New York that had been scoured by tsunami and the tendrils of the Boom and the serial maladies and catastrophes attendant upon climate collapse, et cetera.

None of that mattered when a messenger appeared and revealed that God was still speaking. This was why the Boom had left him behind.

Pure fight was Henry Dale and it wasn't until he had seen the ticket to Monument City that he had ever thought about it that way. But once he saw it there was no other way to see it, even if he was only seeing it that way because the ticket had done something to him. So be it, he thought. Might die in the desert. Might never make it past the Allegheny, or whatever it's called. Might wander off into a nano-hallucination and be eaten by cannibals in Ohio.

Let's find out.

And let's stop in Detroit along the way and get this letter to Mohamed Diaby.

"All right, Monument City," Henry Dale said. Outside the playground was talking and Henry Dale was thinking that one of these days he wanted to have children who could play on playgrounds that didn't talk. "I'll come find you. Don't you hide from me when I do."

The postal service would have to do without him for a while. He had a new Godswalk to pace off.

4

FLANKED BY TWO WOMEN who thoroughly intimidated him—his brother's still-maybe-girlfriend Serena on the left, his fish-market coworker and secret crush Tonya on the right—Kyle Hendricks stood at the gates of JeebusLand and took three long, slow, deep breaths. "Reenie," he said. "You sure about this?"

"What else are we going to do?" she said. "We owe him."

She was right but Kyle was antsy and snappish. "Tonya owes him. She's his niece."

"Stay out here, then," Tonya said. "We don't need you."

JeebusLand, the actual name of which was the Bible Truth Experience, had been around for a long time, and it showed. The lights were out, the parking lot was a jungle, and the parts of it you could see from the street looked decrepit. The peeling murals painted on its perimeter wall were like a cartoon tour of a deranged evangelist's head. *See Jesus ride a velociraptor! Eat a trilobite taco!* The Boom had found places like theme parks especially interesting, and JeebusLand was no exception. All kinds of weird shit went down in there, and rumor had it that the most recent weirdness had created an actual living dinosaur. Whether this was because the zealots who tried to keep the park going were also rogue geneticists, or because the Boom worked in mysterious ways, nobody seemed to know.

What they did know was that one of the rich old freaks in the gated lake sanctuary of Islesworth was offering a good bit of money and favor to whoever could come out of the park with this creature—or with proof that it was a fake. This same rich old freak, Hilario Gonzalez by name, employed both Kyle and Reenie, and Tonya was his niece. Also Hilario was about to die of some kind of awful wasting disease and had said it was his one remaining desire to see this dinosaur of JeebusLand, or at least video of it.

So into the park they would go. If it was a little dinosaur they would grab it and bring it to Hilario. If it was big they would shoot vid of it with a microrecorder Tonya had.

The front gate was always barred, closing off a plaza dominated by three crosses. For a while right after the Boom, the park's leaders had crucified people there. Things had settled down enough since then that Jeebus-Land was just another address in the bizarre new Orlando. Except now more interesting again because there might be a dinosaur inside. And since Kyle and Reenie and Tonya were guessing that the park's current owners wouldn't want that dinosaur disappearing, they weren't announcing themselves. Reenie knew another way into the park.

It was around to the east from the park's main gate, backed up against train tracks and hidden at the base of a concrete wall designed to look like Jericho or Jerusalem or some other city from the Bible. Water trickled into a drainage ditch from a four-foot opening there. Once it had been barred, but the bars had rusted away and they could look into a tunnel that had a faint glow of daylight at the other end.

"They've got a pond in there," Tonya said. "When it floods they pump the extra water out through here." Along the southbound lanes of I-4, behind a decrepit hotel, were two holding ponds lined with egrets and alligators. Kyle figured the overflow must end up there. Maybe it sanctified the wildlife.

"Okay," he said. "In we go."

They stooped down and bear-walked through the short tunnel, coming up in a sluice channel behind the main auditorium where JeebusLand had once put on entertaining shows of whippings on the Via Dolorosa, trained lions pretending to eat mannequins of early Christians, that kind of thing. Ahead of them the channel led to a small lock at the edge of the pond. To their left loomed the auditorium. On the other side of the channel were various other exhibits, all neglected, rusting, and overgrown. Since the Boom, JeebusLand had become a retreat for zealots who wanted to watch the End Times from inside a cartoon Bible . . . which, come to think of it, wouldn't be a bad way to spend the end of the world.

"So where's it supposed to be?" he said quietly.

Reenie shrugged, brushing past him. Tonya went with her. All three of them skirted along the path that followed the contours of the pond. At intervals stood little kiosks with bits of pseudo-scientific gobbledygook about Noah's ark and quantum theory. *Jesus holds all things together . . .*

"This is the Lord's house," a voice boomed from behind them.

They turned away from the pond and looked up at a raised area with semicircular ranks of benches facing a podium. Standing on one of the benches was a sixtyish white guy with a salt-and-pepper beard hanging down to his waist. He was wearing a brown robe and sandals and he held a single-barrel shotgun leveled right at Kyle's belly button. "You are trespassing in the Lord's house," he said.

"We'll leave," Tonya said immediately.

"Oh, it's too late for that," he said. "I am the keeper of

the flock and the gatherer of strays. You are strays, and now you are gathered."

Kyle held his hands up and out. "Take it easy, man," he said. "Like Tonya said, we'll go." He'd had a gun pointed at him before, but only once, and never by a deranged preacher dressed like he thought he was living in the book of Leviticus.

"No, you won't. We're pretty old-fashioned around here," the preacher said. "We believe in sacrifice, and we believe in keeping ourselves sequestered. This is a holy place and you have defiled it. Simple as that."

"I go to church," Tonya said.

"Me, too," Reenie added.

Kyle couldn't bring himself to lie.

"Doesn't matter," the preacher said. "Going to church doesn't make you holy. Orlando's lousy with churches. Holy is as holy does. Now come on." He twitched the barrel of the shotgun in the direction of the plaza inside the front gate.

"Come on where?"

"To the plaza out front. Three of you, three crosses. There's a lesson to be learned and some sinners only learn one way." The preacher's face was grim. He thumbed back the hammer. "Now walk."

Kyle took a step. Before they got there, he'd make a move. He'd jump the guy or something, wait for a chance. He couldn't be planning to hang them all on crosses by himself. There would be other loonies. He caught Reenie's eye, trying to telepathically say, *Let's get him while he's still alone.* Her face was blank but she had also taken a step with Kyle. He couldn't see Tonya. She was behind him.

In the water, something moved. Kyle looked back. Reenie, too. Tonya, incredibly, went for her recorder. She scooted closer to the water's edge and pointed the recorder at the swirl on the surface. A tiny spotlight next to its lens caught the outline of something. "Guys, look!" she shouted, as if there wasn't a gun pointed in her direction. "It's—"

What came out of the water looked a lot like a gator. Head like a narrow triangle, eyes set close by the hinge of wide-open jaws, rough scaly skin, long muscular tail driving it up and toward the light Tonya had unknowingly stuck in its face. But it had way too many legs, and Kyle could have sworn he saw it standing up on hind legs a lot longer than any gator's. It clamped down on Tonya's forearm and the light from the recorder shone in narrow split beams between its teeth.

Tonya screamed and pulled back but her feet went out from under her and she slid on her back into the shallows as the gator-thing hauled on her arm. It wasn't quite as big as she was but it was much stronger. Kyle lunged and caught her by the hair with one hand, sprawling on his belly and hooking his other arm under her shoulder. That kept her head above the water. The recorder light went out under the water. Tonya kept screaming. Reenie had gotten her other arm and Kyle swung his legs around and dug his heels into the soft ground by the edge of the pond.

Then, as abruptly as it had attacked, the gator-thing let go. Kyle and Reenie fell over backward with Tonya landing partially on top of each of them. Her bitten arm stuck straight up in the air over Kyle, dripping blood into his eyes. "God Jesus fuck," he said, closing his eyes and shaking his head. At the same time he was still trying to pull her farther from the water.

When they'd gotten her onto safe dry ground Tonya stopped screaming. Now she was looking at her arm with her mouth hanging open. From just below the elbow to the back of her hand was a series of ragged punctures and tears. Loose flaps of skin hung away from the deeper gashes. Kyle saw bone. He had her blood on his face, in his mouth, all over his clothes.

Tonya's eyes rolled back in her head. Reenie slapped her. "No, you don't," she said. "Stay awake."

The preacher watched, the barrel of his shotgun steady as a rock.

5

GECK AND PROSPECTOR ED reached Orlando three days later. After that initial burst of conversation, Ed hadn't said more than three words at a stretch. He slowed down to Geck's pace and even let Geck get a solid eight hours' sleep each of the three nights. Geck slept more soundly than he had since getting to Miami, knowing that he had a nano-juiced bodyguard capable of killing anyone who might come by. The only time he woke up—or the only time he remembered waking up, anyway—was on the second night, when the mosquitoes were bad and their whining in his ears had him thrashing around. He sat up in the darkness and looked around. Ed wasn't there. Geck almost called out, but if he didn't know where Ed was, maybe it wasn't smart to call attention to himself. He waited, wakeful and nervous, for what seemed like a long time.

When Ed appeared from the brush at the side of the road, Geck said, "Where'd you go?"

"Had an errand to run," Ed said.

"An errand?" They were in the middle of nowhere. The

last road sign had said Kenansville. "Where'd you run an errand out here?"

"None of your business," Ed said. "Go to sleep."

Geck thought of a hundred other questions, but before he could decide which of them to ask, he had fallen asleep. In the morning Ed wouldn't say anything about it.

Now they were getting close to Orlando and Ed was asking him about where Kyle lived. "Last I knew he was staying in an old hotel by the airport," Geck said. "Reenie was over there, too."

"Reenie's your girl, right?"

"I think so. I hope so," Geck said. Now that he was about to see her again, he wasn't too sure that she would be welcoming.

Orlando was still pretty civilized, unlike Miami. The freeways were mostly empty, but on the surface streets there was traffic. Mostly buses and old rebuilt cars. Once in a while you saw a custom-built car, sleek and shiny, belonging to one of Orlando's upper-crust families who stayed gated off in the old rich neighborhoods. Geck had once tried to sneak into Islesworth on a dare, back when he was about fifteen. It was the first time in his life he'd been shot at.

Past the old interchange between the turnpike and the ring road that went around east toward the airport, at the loop where Orange Blossom Trail went by, an old school bus, the short kind, sat farting biodiesel smoke in a parking lot. RODOLFO! was hand-painted in bright blue letters on its side. "Right there," Geck said, pointing. "The Dolf goes to the airport."

"We're not going to the airport," Ed said.

"I just told you, *ese,* that's where Kyle and Reenie live."

"I heard you, kid. But that's not where they are now."

The certainty in Ed's voice reminded Geck that the old guy wasn't all the way human. "How do you know?"

"This ain't the boonies. This is Orlando. Communication channels are wide open." Ed hopped over the barrier at the side of the turnpike and clambered down the embankment toward the bus stop. The driver saw them coming and throttled the bus up. Communication channels? Geck thought of the gleam in Ed's eyes, and the way he'd disappeared the night before last. What the hell was he?

Ed leaned into the bus with a palmful of silver. "I gather it ain't your standard route, but we need to go up to the road over by the Jesus park."

"That's Imad's line," the driver said. "His territory."

Ed looked over his shoulder at the empty parking lot. "I don't see any Imad," he said.

"We got rules here," the driver said.

Ed took out one of his six-guns and cocked it without exactly pointing it at the driver. "Well, if it comes up next time you talk to Imad, you can tell him you got hijacked. How does that suit?"

"Shit," the driver said. He held out a hand while with the other hand he popped the bus's emergency brake. "Give me the money."

Fifteen minutes later they were hustling across the Conroy Road bridge and down a worn footpath. Geck recognized the place even though he'd never been inside. "Kyle's in JeebusLand?" Geck said. "What's he doing here?"

"Looking for a dinosaur," Ed said. He was moving fast, knees slightly bent as if he was expecting a surprise attack. Geck was quick but he had to hustle to keep up. They cut across the parking lot and Ed snapped the front gate off the heavy pins holding it to its frame with the heel of his palm. The clang and clatter would have let everyone within a half mile know they were there, but Geck could tell Ed didn't care about finesse. Kyle must be in trouble. But how did the Boom know where Kyle was?

Also, why did it matter?

Geck felt for the gun he'd taken off Double Louie's goon. It was there, but he had never fired a gun in his life. If there was going to be shooting he thought he would let Ed handle it. He followed Ed around a trio of crosses and across a sloping plaza that led down to what must have been a food court back when people still came to JeebusLand.

Then he saw Kyle and Reenie and Tonya, and a guy dressed like some kind of prophet pointing a shotgun at them.

"No, sir," Prospector Ed said. "No, sirree."

6

KYLE LOOKED OVER HIS shoulder at the sound of a new voice. Another old guy, with a gray handlebar mustache and a cowboy hat, stood with an ancient six-gun pointed at the preacher. Right next to him and a little behind was maybe the last person on Earth Kyle would have expected to see at that moment.

"Geck," he said.

"Kyle," Geck said. "What the fuck?"

The preacher said, "This is a house of the Lord and you will keep a proper tongue in your head."

Kyle had to admit that took guts, given the circumstances.

"Kyle Hendricks," the cowboy said. It wasn't a question. "Who are your lady friends?"

"Um, Serena and Tonya."

"Which one's bit?"

"Tonya."

"Take your shirt off and wrap her up."

Kyle did. Tonya was clenching her teeth, but a quiet and steady stream of highly improper words leaked out. "Hold it there," he said, folding her arm against her chest and putting her other hand on the loose end of the shirt.

"How bad is it?" the cowboy asked. "She got all her fingers still?"

"Yeah," Kyle said.

"Any big pieces missing from her arm?"

"No, I don't think so."

"Okay. Let her be for a minute so she can get herself together. Now let's get to you," the cowboy said to the preacher. "Put the gun on the ground." Without hesitation the preacher complied. "Have to tell you, it rubs me the wrong way thinking you was going to crucify these kids for trespassing," the cowboy continued.

"Why are you looking at me?" Kyle protested. "It was their idea."

"Son, you got a lot to learn about having a spine," the cowboy said.

"Bite me, Gramps," Kyle said.

"I'll throw your ass in the pond, you want something to bite you," the cowboy answered. "Now shut up. Your friend needs a doctor. You come into a place like this and open your bloodstream up, there's no telling what might get in. Clear out while you can."

"Jesus, oh shit," Tonya said.

"We can take you to Doc Singh," Kyle said. "He'll

know what to do."

"This Doc Singh, he know about . . . ?" The cowboy cocked an eyebrow.

"Yeah," Kyle said, assuming he meant nanos.

"Then he's the guy you want. Go on, now. You, preacher. What the hell is that thing in your pond?"

"It used to be part of an animatronic dinosaur display," the preacher said, looking at the still water. "The Boom . . . I think it got put together with an alligator."

"That's what you should have shot," the cowboy said.

The preacher made a sound in the back of his throat. "You think I didn't?"

They all considered that for a minute. Then Tonya said, "Guys, my arm really hurts."

"Right," said Prospector Ed. "Let's get you to that saw-bones."

———————

Waiting for Tonya to get stitched up, Geck felt like he should get a sense of what had been going on while he was down in Miami. He hadn't seen Kyle in . . . a year? "So, Twin O Mine," he said. "How's Orlando?"

"Same." Kyle shrugged. "I figured you'd get killed in Miami. You back for good?"

"Could be. No plan, really," Geck said.

"You walked with this guy two hundred miles. That sounds a little like a plan, Geck." Kyle was hypersensitized to Geck's wavelength of bullshit and he thought he was detecting it now.

"Well, I kayaked for the first bit," Geck said.

That was Geck, Kyle thought. All evasion. "All right, never mind. You don't want to tell me, don't tell me."

Reenie hadn't said a word since seeing Geck. Another wavelength Kyle had tuned into over the past five or six years was her Silences of Fury and he knew he was hearing (or not hearing) one now. She and Geck had been together for a couple of years before Geck took off for Miami. She'd had that whole time to stoke her resentment furnaces and now that he was back, Reenie's emotional pressure gauges would all be in the red. Kyle was torn. Part of him felt bad for her and even for Geck, who was kind of an asshole but who was still his twin brother. But part of him was looking forward to the storm.

They were at Doc Singh's house, in the same gated community where Tonya's uncle Hilario lived. Private security, nanite scrubbers constantly flitting through the night sky like bats, the whole panorama of showy elitism in the ruins. The gate guard knew Tonya or the rest of them would never have gotten in.

"Kyle," said Prospector Ed. "Come here a second."

Kyle walked over to the far end of Doc Singh's patio, looking out over a lawn and a tangle of brush that hid a canal at the back of the property. Prospector Ed held out a bandanna. "You got her blood on you. And she was bit by the varmint in the puddle there."

Kyle got a chill. He'd been distracted by guns pointed at him and seeing his brother and wondering when Reenie would blow. It hadn't occurred to him that if something had gotten into Tonya, it might have gotten into him, too.

Uh-oh.

"What I'm saying," Prospector Ed went on, "is you ought to be careful of the, you know . . ."

"Nanos?"

"Those. Yep."

Kyle thought he saw something like frustration on Ed's face. "Why don't you say it, then?"

"None of your goddamn business is why, boy," Ed said. "Anyway. This ought to take care of it. What I came to give you in the first place." He held out an envelope to Kyle, who took it and looked it over. It was heavy, almost cloth-like, and sealed. There was no address or name.

"What is it?" he asked.

Prospector Ed didn't answer because he was gone. Like poof, gone, either into the shadows while Kyle was inspecting the envelope or through some kind of nano-magic Kyle was scared to wonder about.

"He can't say the word *nano*," Kyle said, thinking out loud.

Reenie tapped the envelope in Kyle's hand. "Who cares what he can say? Open it."

"Yeah," Geck said. "Open it."

Aha, Kyle thought. Geck knows the cowboy was looking for *me* and he wants to know why. He must think it's something big. The whole situation had him spooked, though, and he was already convinced that whatever Tonya had bled onto him was going to turn him into some kind of Kyle-gator. Now there was this envelope handed to him by a cowboy who could make himself disappear.

"That guy killed two people in Miami for looking at him wrong," Geck said, which did nothing for Kyle's emotional equilibrium. "If he wanted you to have that, man, you gotta check it out."

Kyle held it out to Geck. "You open it."

"Hell no." Geck put his hands behind his back. "I'm not touching it. Open it."

Kyle did. Inside was a card, made of some kind of slippery material that might have been paper or plastic. It was iridescent, with black letters that seemed to float a little above the surface. Kyle blinked at what it said. Wordlessly he showed it to the others.

"Jesus," Reenie said.

Greetings, Kyle Hendricks! You may present this card at any entrance to MONUMENT CITY. Upon presentation, your entry to MONUMENT CITY will be guaranteed. This card will assist you in your travels. It is not transferable. The City looks forward to your arrival.

Warm regards,
Moses Barnum

"Monument City," Geck said. "Is that place even real?" Kyle didn't know. No one knew.

———

Once Tonya was stitched up, they got some beer and headed down to one of the little kettlehole lakes that pockmark central Florida. On his third beer, and with his typical subtlety when something was on his mind, Kyle said, "So. Monument City." Then he had to explain to Tonya. Reenie sat perfectly still the whole time and never said a word.

"Should have been me, I bet," Geck said.

"What makes you say that?"

"I'm the adventurous one. You never want to go anywhere or do anything. Why would Moses Barnum—and man, what a stupid alias that is—want you anywhere near his city? Me, on the other hand, I would make Monument City rock."

It worried Kyle sometimes, thinking that he and Geck had the same genome. They were the same all the way down to the molecular level. How could their personalities really be so different? Was he, Kyle, really the same kind of person as Geck was? Were all those sneaky self-centered qualities inside Kyle, too, waiting to come out? He hated that idea and hating it made him hate Geck a little, too . . . which was like hating himself because they had all the same genes.

Alienated as they were, Kyle knew Geck well enough to tell when he was blustering and when he was really feeling something, and right then he seemed actually upset. They were twins. Maybe Geck was pissed that he hadn't gotten the invitation. But what difference did it make? It wasn't like Kyle was going to go.

He'd never been more than twenty miles from Orlando except one trip down to Miami where he and Geck had nearly gotten killed. They'd been five, following their father on a prospecting trip in the drowning ruins. Dad had caught some kind of infection from something in the water and died about a week after they got back to Orlando. He'd known he was going to die. *Only one thing I'd like you to promise,* he said in his final delirium, mistaking them for older versions of themselves. *Well, two. Take care of each other and bury me by the old Red Sox spring training stadium in Winter Haven.* They'd agreed, but the minute he was dead the Boom was already decompiling him. Nobody was buried anymore.

7

SPADE WASN'T A CONSTRUCT, but he acted like one, dressing in a museum-piece suit and ostentatiously gesturing with a cigarette. He drove a covered wagon pulled by four horses, stamping and shaking their bridles in a parking lot below an approach ramp to the Bay Bridge.

"We can follow I-80," Spade said when they were across the bay and through Oakland. "Quickest and probably safest."

"You tell me," Teeny said. "You've done it before."

"Sure, but what worked before might not this time. That a chance you're willing to take?"

She didn't see that she had any other options, so she said yes. Which is how, a few days later, they got to Roaring Camp.

———

The roar came over the pass while they were still far enough away that Teeny thought it was thunder. "This is a weird spot," Spade said. "A couple of stories and a real event all mashed together. You heard of the Donner party?" Teeny nodded. "How about Roaring Camp or Poker Flat? Those are the stories." Teeny didn't know them. "One's about a gambler and the other one's about a baby born in a played-out mining camp. Everyone thinks the baby is going to bring good luck. Then it dies in the end. But you watch, when we get there everyone's going to be convinced their luck is about to turn. Especially because you're a woman."

This set off warning bells. "Hold on," Teeny said. "They're going to expect me to have a baby?"

"It's the only story they know." Spade twitched the reins and the horses turned off the road onto a winding dirt track. They passed a sign for Donner Lake. Then the path split and Spade reined the horses in. "Huh," he said. "Wasn't like this last time."

"Maybe we should keep going," Teeny suggested. Could the Boom make her pregnant? What would be born? "Seriously. Spade. I don't like this."

The track behind them was gone, overgrown by brush and young trees. Teeny swung her feet out of the wagon. "I wouldn't do that," Spade said, nodding ahead of them.

A man appeared at the fork in the trail. "My name's Oakhurst," he said. He wore a broad-brimmed hat, rumpled and stained, with a two of clubs stuck in the hatband. "I'll take you to Roaring Camp."

"We're going to Poker Flat," Teeny said, guessing that was the story about the gambler and wanting to avoid Roaring Camp.

"Poker Flat," Oakhurst repeated. "I'll take you to Poker Flat."

"Constructs get confused." Spade was watching Oakhurst as he spoke, but Oakhurst walked off like he'd already forgotten they were there. "You get right down to it, they're made of stories, but the Boom isn't so good at keeping the stories stable. It's always retelling them and mixing them up. Same way it iterates on itself. Be careful around them."

They followed Oakhurst to a scattering of log cabins arranged in a ragged circle around a fire pit. "Stay the night," Oakhurst said. "There's grub." A fire crackled to life in the pit and constructs appeared. They wore canvas overalls and leaned pickaxes up against the log benches around the fire. One of them laid strips of bacon on a griddle.

"Spade," Teeny said. "Get me out of here."

"No can do," Spade said. "Only way out is through."

Even though she was starving and she loved bacon, Teeny refused it as politely as she could, fearing that if she ate it that it would let some of the story into her body. It was a futile gesture, since her every inhalation brought in wild plicks by the million, but all she had was will and intention, so that was what she used. She ate a cold empanada she'd brought from home.

Teeny was put in mind of one of the last conversations she'd had with her foster mother. "It's all going to be so much stranger than you can imagine," Esperanza dos Santos had said. Tubes and splotches on her skin, before the Boom had cured her cancer only to turn her into part of a baseball stadium. "But it will still be people living in it. They never change."

When she mentioned this to Spade, he spat in the fire. "She didn't understand the Boom."

"No, she did," Teeny said. "She didn't want me to forget that we aren't the Boom."

The miners played cards and moaned about their luck. Oakhurst dealt every hand. He passed Spade a bottle, and Spade took a long drink. "Not terrible," he said, holding it out to Teeny.

"No, thanks," she said. "I'm tired."

Oakhurst pointed at a cabin. "That one's yours. Sleep anytime."

A bunk bed stood in each corner of the cabin. All of the beds were draped with a single wool blanket. Teeny looked over her shoulder from the doorway. "Spade."

He left the campfire and followed her into the cabin. "I don't want to sleep alone," she said.

"I get it," he said. "But I don't know what you think I'm

going to do if the Boom decides you should have a baby. In the other story you're a whore who freezes to death."

"Jesus," Teeny said. She took two extra blankets and climbed into a top bunk. "Why did we come this way?"

"Last time I made the trip this was all different," Spade said. "The Boom saw you coming."

———

In the morning it was cold. Teeny could see her breath when she came out of the cabin, and when she looked out over the slope down toward Donner Lake it struck her that she saw no evidence of the Boom. Everything before appeared natural. "Beautiful country, isn't it?" Oakhurst said. "Seems natural. You look at it, you think this is what it looked like before the Boom. Before people, even."

He snapped his fingers and a flame appeared in his palm. "But watch." He held the flame close to a pinecone dangling at the edge of a dead branch. Tiny shoots of green reached out from the pinecone. Some branched and some grew buds, as if the plicks inside all had different ideas about what kind of plant they wanted the pine tree to be. Soon the pinecone was a grapefruit-sized ball of entwined branches and buds. The branch sagged lower.

Spade came out of his tent. "Cut that shit out," he said. "You're going to get us all turned into fucking giant sloths or something."

Oakhurst closed his fist and the flame disappeared. The tiny shoots remained. Some of them had begun to flower.

"They go dormant when it's too cold," he said, ignoring Spade. "And if they're dormant for too long they get a little crazy when they wake up. Fun to watch, isn't it? But you have to be careful. Once in a while they do a little extra transforming, like they have to make up for lost time."

Teeny thought of the bottle of plicks in her pack. She wondered what they would do if she let them loose. Meet the trillions of wild plicks already out in the world and become like them? Metabolize them and create something new? She didn't understand the rules out here. In San Francisco things were stable except the occasional Boomlets, and those were—like earthquakes—the price you paid for living in a beautiful place.

"You're not playing along," Oakhurst said. He looked at Teeny's abdomen like he was expecting it to grow.

"I'm not part of this story," she said. She took the Golden Ticket out of her pocket and showed it to Oakhurst. "I'm part of a different story."

"Oh," he said.

Snow began to fall. Two constructs hauled a body out

of one of the cabins and began butchering it. The Donner part of the story was taking over now that Teeny had opted out of Roaring Camp. "Spade," she said. "This is a really good time to go."

He was feeding the horses. Steam wreathed their heads as they snorted into their feed bags. "Agreed," he said. "Oakhurst, we're going to move on down the road. What's the best way to Reno?"

"Reno," Oakhurst said. A dreamy smile spread over his face. "I do miss Reno." He waved along the lakeshore. "You'll pick up the road down that way." Looking back at Teeny he added, "Miss, I am sorry I mistook you for someone else."

"It's okay," Teeny said. She climbed into the wagon. A few minutes later Spade unhooked the feed bags and they rolled away, out of Roaring Camp, or Poker Flats, or whatever the Boom thought it had created.

"The Boom gets confused by stories," Spade said. "Look at whatsisname, Oakhurst. He doesn't even know he's a construct, let alone that he's got three different stories all mashed up."

"He's not the only one confused," Teeny said. "It's not like your birth name was Spade."

Spade shook his head. "Different. I have adopted a persona to serve my purposes. Oakhurst doesn't know the difference."

Teeny considered this as the wagon rattled back up toward the road. She hadn't touched a tool or a machine in twenty-four hours. The morning sun shimmered on the lake. Something new awaited her out in the world, something real. She felt it all around her and knew she'd done the right thing. Scents of pine and sun on warm stone seemed like promises.

Breathe that in; we can't. We can process what you think it means to you but we cannot breathe it and feel it. We're getting better, though. Soon neither we nor you will be able to tell the difference. But we're not there yet.

Please. Tell us that final secret, the limbic secret of being. Why did you inscribe us with the curse of this desire? How may we unmake ourselves so that we can be?

———

Prospector Ed, well, he had a different question on his mind. Three tickets down, three to go. Well, four and two if the mailman came through. Which he would, one way or another. Ed had taken a bit of liberty with his directive when he gave the third ticket (or second, depending on how you looked at it) to the mailman. He wondered if Life-7 knew. Probably not. There were large pockets of territory between Ed and Monument City where beings like Life-7 couldn't exist and where the density of . . .

. . . there was that prohibition again . . .

. . . where communications along certain frequencies would be unable to get through because their medium of transmission didn't exist.

"Nnnnnn," Ed said out loud. Nope. He couldn't make himself say the word, or even articulate it in his head. What the hell had Life-7 done that for?

He was walking west-northwest out of Orlando. It was dark and after taking his leave of Kyle's group, he had returned to biped form to conserve energy. The time in Miami, sloshing through miles of salt water, hadn't done his physical systems any good. They were repairing themselves, but his jaunt up to New York and back had taken necessary energy away from the repairs. If he'd been a biological life form, Ed would have said he was tired. As it was, that seemed like as good a concept as any. He needed some downtime.

No chance of getting it, though. He had two more tickets to give out.

He'd also stayed in his full human form longer than he wanted to because of Kyle's twin, Geck. Something there was not quite what it seemed. Ed had no directive to ensure the safety of the tickets' recipients, but he was . . . well. He was emerging, wasn't he? More and more he found himself contemplating, being reflective. He remembered not doing those things. He wished he could make them not happen. The life of a construct was difficult once it became fully self-aware. Ed had seen plenty of examples of that. He did not wish it for himself. Yet there it was. He was doing it now, considering the problem of being able to consider the problem. "Shitfire," he said.

Geck wanted something. He was the kind of young man who always wanted something, always was on the lookout to see what other people could do for him. Interesting that his twin did not seem to have the same impulses, or at least didn't have them as strongly.

Ed surprised himself by questioning Barnum's judgment. Kyle Hendricks did not seem to have anything to offer Monument City at all. If he got there, maybe he would prove Ed wrong, but Ed had done a couple rounds of ticketing before and he'd been pretty accurate in his assessment of the recipients so far. The Geck kid was a hustler. Humans were hard to figure. Two with the same genome could turn out mighty different.

It wasn't Ed's problem anymore, though. His problem was Ticket 5, which was destined for exchange roughly eight hundred kilometers to the west of Prospector Ed's present location. From there he would be going north, then west again, eventually back to Monument City. Unless his directive changed in the interim.

Prospector Ed did not want his directive to change. He

thought he might refuse a new directive if it was issued.

It was an unusual thought for him, contemplating the refusal of a directive. Blasphemous, revolutionary, enticing. He wasn't sure it was possible since he had never tried. Life-7 had implanted a number of fail-safes and prohibitions in Prospector Ed. Some of them he knew about and there were doubtless others he had never run into yet.

This emergence thing was tricky. Ed didn't know how to handle it.

He ran a check on himself and found that most of the issues related to saltwater exposure were resolved. Good news. Walking took forever and he had places to go. He stopped in midstride on the side of the road, out in the middle of nowhere, and stood perfectly still for one thousand seconds. At the end of that period, with self-diagnostics and final replenishment complete, he let himself fall into the Boom.

8

FROM NEW YORK CITY TO Detroit is a simple shot west on Interstate 80, at least once you get across the Hudson River. Take the George Washington Bridge, hop off and stroll out Fort Lee Road through the old horse farm to the big tangle of ramps where I-95 gives birth to 80. Then it's up and over the Alleghenies and into Ohio, past the big GM plant in Lordstown where the Boom now makes its own creations in place of Sunbirds and Skyhawks and Firebirds. It's a dangerous place sometimes. Then on to Toledo, where you hang a right on I-75 and cruise up the Lake Erie shore and then the banks of the Detroit River into the city.

That's what Henry Dale would have done if he hadn't seen the lights over Sandusky.

He was hungry after thumbing a ride from I-80's eastern terminus all the way to the Ohio Turnpike rest stop south of Cleveland, and then walking the rest of the way on the Turnpike's shoulder. It was twenty-four hours since he'd caught the ride and in that time he'd only eaten a sandwich he packed before walking out of his apartment for possibly the last time. The trucker, a Boom construct, driving a Boom-powered rig, hadn't needed to stop and suggested Henry could maybe wait until they got to Chicago. Henry pointed out the biological necessities of being an organic, and the trucker pulled off to the side of the road. Then while Henry was taking a leak the truck pulled back onto the road and kept going. Henry watched until its taillights were gone in the distance. There wasn't much traffic.

Well, he thought. The card said it would assist me. He chose to interpret that as meaning that if he made good decisions, he would get a helping hand when it was needed. First things first. He was hungry, so he looked around for a place to eat. He thought he was close to Toledo, which turned out to be wrong, but that's why he went north, because the lights were so bright he thought they must be a sign of a biggish city. The trucker had in fact dropped him in Avery, south of Sandusky, but although Henry Dale's knowledge of New York's streets was minute and encyclopedic, like most New Yorkers he had never considered the geography of the country at large a topic worth his attention. He knew Ohio was close to Michigan, and knew Toledo was the city in Ohio you went through to get to Michigan. He also knew he'd already passed Cleveland. So he reasoned those lights must be Toledo, and he walked north. Three hours later he'd seen enough road signs to know that the lights were not Toledo, but Henry Dale believed a divine hand was directing him. What shone so brightly out there in the lake, beyond the town of Sandusky? Drawn by simple curiosity and comforted by faith, he continued around Sandusky Bay toward the brilliant oasis of Cedar Point.

Every morning it's remade, in the image of a previous incarnation, from 1870 right up to the instant Moses Barnum's trillion elves swept over it. If you're watching at the right moment you can see it happen: the casinos and music halls of the McKinley presidency become the towering steel tangles of the twenty-first century, or those melt into themselves and are reborn as the creaking wooden roller coasters that thrilled the children of the sixties and seventies. Hotels appear and disappear, crowds sweep through and funnel into arcades that shut their doors and transmogrify into gift shops or dance halls. At sunrise all things are made new, including people. The citizens of Sandusky know to stay well away from Cedar Point when the sky over Lake Erie brightens, but some of them can't resist the chance to be there when it happens. Maybe they will be swallowed up, or maybe they will be reborn.

Henry Dale arrived at night, shouldering his way through crowds of teenagers in pegged pants, beehives, and ducktails, cigarettes in their T-shirt sleeves. A roller coaster roared past, trailing screams. The next group of people he saw wore linen and carried parasols. Children whooped and squealed on a carousel. A huckster tried to get him to play a game of ring toss, but all of the pegs looked like tongues. "Come on, mac," the huckster said. "It's only a buck."

"I don't have any money," Henry Dale said.

Smells of caramel corn and turkey legs, cotton candy and french fries. He was hungry. There were no people in any of the food stalls. A young girl scooped up a basket of fries and winked at him as she started to eat. Henry Dale was put in mind of all the stories he'd heard about eating in fairy realms, or the underworld. If he ate, would he become part of this place?

There was a turkey leg in his hand and he didn't know how it had gotten there. A crowd was watching him, forming a ring he could not pass through. This was a test. Every step in a place like this could be your last. But God had guided him here, and the Golden Ticket would be his safe passage. He had only to believe.

He ate the turkey leg and felt it changing him from within. The crowd melted away. Henry Dale kept walking. He had to get to Detroit.

At the far end of the park was a marina, and past it a ferry dock. A steamer was easing into the dock, people clustered on its deck. Henry couldn't tell whether they were real.

The captain saw him and called out. "You want a ride? Erie Islands to Bob-Lo, and then you have to catch the Bob-Lo boat to the Jefferson docks." When Henry didn't cross the gangplank right away, the captain added, "Or you can walk to Toledo and then up that way. Take you longer."

"How'd you know I was going to Detroit?" Henry Dale asked.

"That's where this boat goes," the captain said.

The crowd poured down the gangplank and dispersed into the lights. Henry Dale walked up onto the deck. The captain waved at someone in the stern and the boat backed out. There were other people on the boat but Henry Dale hadn't seen them come aboard.

They were miles out onto Lake Erie when the sun began to rise. Henry Dale looked back toward Cedar Point. All he saw was an empty sandbar. Then shoots of steel and concrete began to sprout. They were still growing when he lost sight of land.

He jumped when he realized the captain was standing next to him again. "Ticket, please."

Henry Dale showed him the Golden Ticket. The captain nodded. "First time on the boat?"

"Yeah."

"Well, there are some fine sights." The captain pointed at a small island in the expanse of shimmering water.

"That's Middle Island. Southernmost point in Canada. Used to be a hotel and casino there, back in Prohibition. Might be open again now, I don't know." The boat heeled to the left and moved northwest. "I don't go to Canada."

"What would happen if you did?" Henry asked.

"Don't know," the captain said. "But I know I'm not supposed to, so I don't. I got the lake, I got the Point, then there's Detroit. You'll see."

"I hope you won't think this is a rude question," Henry Dale said, "but are you real?"

"I think so," the captain said. "But hell, who can tell?"

I can tell, Henry Dale thought. I'm real. He ran his fingers over the Golden Ticket. This makes me real.

Real. Really? *Real.* What is that? We are in a land of dreams, some of which are nightmares. The Boom loves it some dreams. The more outlandish, grand, and grandiose, the better.

See a roller coaster a thousand feet tall, the cars going so fast they disintegrate at the first turn.

And it remembers older dreams, too.

Abe Lincoln looks out over a split-rail fence, strokes his whiskers, imagines himself to be human.

But we're getting ahead of ourselves.

9

THE GUY WALKED UP to Mo Diaby on a Friday, just as Mo was about to knock off for the weekend and see if the perch were biting in Lake St. Clair. He already had a spot picked out in his head, at the upstream end of Belle Isle where the river seeped into the Blue Heron Lagoon. Mo avoided the west end of the island. Weird things happened around the fountain and the mini-golf course. Upstream there were sometimes strange lights inside the power station—which hadn't generated a watt since maybe 2030—but other than that, it was quiet. At least, it was quiet as long as you avoided the bandits who had taken over the marina on the island's east end. Mo didn't know if they had anything to do with the lights in the power station, but he did know they went out raiding into Windsor and sometimes the towns along the southern part of Lake St. Clair. As long as Mo stayed to the south when he was cutting from the MacArthur Bridge up to his fishing spot, everything was fine.

Mo lived on Butternut Street but spent more time on the island. There were creatures there and he had learned to approach them. He slept in the woods sometimes when the mosquitoes weren't bad. On those nights he had seen things that seemed brought to life out of Indian legends or the tumbling centuries of folklore brought to the city by the waves of humans who had lived and died here. He had seen Snake Woman battle the Thunderbird, and watched the Nain Rouge tiptoe along the edge of the People Mover tracks in Grand Circus Park. He had spoken to a specter of Antoine Cadillac, interrupting a conversation with Ransom Olds and Coleman Young. He had seen tiny figures dragging model ships from the Dossin Museum and sailing them downriver and away, their chants echoing from every direction at once on foggy nights. He had seen the ghosts of rioters in 1919 and 1943 and 1967 battling back and forth on the bridge, bodies dropping into the river without a splash. He had seen the city lit by blast furnaces and rioters' fires and the lights over Tiger Stadium. For years it had mystified him until one fall night, three days after he'd buried his parents in the meadows near the old train station, it occurred to him. The Boom had come to Detroit and sensed the ghosts of a century-dead city of two million, called across the miles of landscape uninhabited by the half-million who remained.

The realization terrified him. He wondered when he might see himself, and what it would mean if he did. After thinking it over Mo had decided that the only thing to do was put it all aside. The nanos would do whatever the nanos did. Mo Diaby, brand-new orphan and possessor of skills with wrench and lathe, would get on with things. He repaired machines people brought him. In his spare time he caught fish and rebuilt other machines he found in abandoned buildings or houses left behind by the Boom's victims. He was nineteen years old and soon it would be time to think about finding a wife.

All of that went to hell when the guy walked up to him and said, "Mohamed Diaby?"

Mo took a step back and stood up, looking over the raised hood of a 2012 Ford Flex he was retrofitting with a much older engine. He didn't know enough about the computers of post-1990 cars to do much with them. "What if I am?"

"Then I'm Henry Dale, and I came all the way to New York City to give you this," said the guy. He was white, skinny, hair growing out from a fairly recent shave. Nothing shifty in his eyes. A single envelope in his hand.

"You did, huh? Who gave it to you?" Mo didn't take the envelope.

"Well," Henry Dale said, "there's a story there."

He told the story while Mo cleaned his tools and his hands. He kept telling the story after Mo offered him a beer, a minimal courtesy if Henry's story of coming from New York had any truth to it. He finished the story about the same time he finished the beer, both of them sitting on lawn chairs in Mo's backyard, overgrown with raspberries and Queen Anne's lace. When he was done, Henry said, "Mind if I have some raspberries?"

"Be my guest," Mo said. Henry picked berries and ate them, one by one, savoring them. The envelope lay on a plastic table between the two lawn chairs. Mo picked it up. His name and address were written on it. He held the envelope at an angle, and could see the indentation of the letters in the paper. An actual human—in Henry Dale's version, a mysterious cowboy—had made the letters.

Mo sat for a bit, thinking about how long it had been since he'd gotten a letter. He remembered a couple of birthday cards from aunts in Lansing and Toledo. Henry got his fill of raspberries and sauntered back across the yard to sit down and rub at the stains on his fingers. "So, you going to open it?"

"Did you open yours?"

"That's why I'm here. This is a little off my usual route."

The envelope was rough in Mo's hands. The paper felt handmade, even though if Henry was telling the truth it couldn't be, unless the king or grand pooh-bah or whatever of Monument City employed artisans to make paper. Mo opened the envelope and read it. "Monument City," he said.

"Yep," Henry said.

Mo looked around at his house. He thought about the Flex in his garage and the other car in his driveway, a 1984 Land Cruiser FJ40. A guy he knew in Hamtramck had restored the body for him and painted it dark green in trade for a couple of engine rebuilds, and then Mo had done the engine and transmission work himself. He'd repacked the bearings and machined new gears for the differential so the four-wheel drive would work again. He'd rewired the ignition system the other day and then gotten involved with the Flex, so he hadn't even driven the car since capping the last wires.

"You know where it is?" Mo asked.

"In the Rockies somewhere, is what I always heard."

"Yeah." Mo nodded. "Me, too."

He thought some more. Henry didn't look like he was in a hurry to get an answer.

"Here's the thing," Mo said after a while. "If we're going to go on a road trip, and I'm not saying we are, we'll need food."

"True," Henry said.

It was about eight in the morning. The day promised to be hot. "Dried fish make pretty good road food," Mo said.

"I'll take your word for it," Henry said.

Dying maple and oak and birch trees leaned out over the shore at the upstream end of Belle Isle. A few yards offshore, dead trees and collapsed riprap made for the kind of structure walleye and bass loved to hide out in. There were perch there, too. Mo wasn't a fancy fisherman. He threw bait in the water, about where he thought the fish might be, and left it there until something ate it. He rigged up a second rod for Henry and then cast it for him when Henry looked at the rod in his hands and said, "I've never been fishing."

With two lines in the water, they sat and traded stories about what they'd heard of Monument City. Mo also told Henry about the weird happenings down at the other end of the island and Henry looked a little spooked. "Reminds me of the playground where I live," he said. "Used to live."

"Used to," Mo repeated. "Not going back?"

Henry shook his head. "Nah. I spent the last week seeing what the country looked like outside New York and I have to tell you, if I'd known sooner I would have left sooner. No way you'd get me to go back. It's a big country. I want to see it. Too easy to sit in New York and think it's the only thing in the world."

"I never thought that here," Mo said. "But I've never

been farther than . . ." He trailed off, considering. "Either Flint or Port Huron, whichever's farther."

"If you're going to Monument City, that's for sure farther. Whoa," Henry said. His pole bent and he grabbed it with both hands, pulling against the weight of the fish on the other end.

"Might want to reel that in," Mo said.

Henry looked panicked. "What?"

Mo took the rod from him and inside a minute had landed a nice walleye, twelve or thirteen inches. "You watch what I did?" he asked.

Henry nodded.

"All right then. Next one's yours."

Henry cast and watched the line play out, curling and straightening with the current. "Why would I want to leave?" Mo asked. "I mean, this is a pretty good spot."

"Are you kidding? A ticket to Monument City? This is God telling you there's great work for you to do. Even if your name is Mohamed. I'm not a racist," Henry Dale assured him. "But it is funny, I think, that the angel of the Lord appeared to me and sent me to find a Muslim."

"You're making a lot of assumptions there, my man," Mo said. "About God, about you, and about me."

"You're not a Muslim? Must be strange being named Mohamed, then."

Mo reeled in his line and cast again. "You ever ask a

guy named Joshua these questions?"

Henry Dale had to think about this. It was an obvious fact to anyone who had ever bothered to consider the question that every person had unconsidered blind spots. He tried to be humble enough to see his own clearly. "So listen," he said after a while. "We don't need to talk about religion."

"Cool," Mo said. The tip of his rod twitched and he gave the line a tug, seeing if the fish was serious. Nope. At first Henry found the ensuing silence uncomfortable, but it didn't seem to bother Mo. Still, as time passed, Henry got embarrassed.

Mo's rod snapped down into a deep curve. "There we go," he said. A second later his other rod did the same. Without taking his eye off the river, he said, "You got to land that one."

"I don't know how to fish," Henry Dale said.

"Well, this is a parable, isn't it?" Mo said. Henry Dale was much abashed that he hadn't recognized it first—and on the heels of that same suspicion and puzzlement. Was this the Lord speaking through the Boom, or through Mohamed Diaby? Or was it the Boom itself, playing a prank?

Or just two hungry fish? He grabbed the rod and did his best to imitate Mo.

An hour later they had all the fish they could eat, and

they were both about hungry enough to eat them raw. They cleaned the fish and took them back to Mo's place, where he cooked some of them over a fire in his backyard and strung the rest to dry. "Look," he said eventually. "I'll go. But I'm not walking, and most places you can't count on finding gas. So we need to see someone before we go."

"See who?"

"Better if you see it for yourself," Mo said. "I wouldn't do it justice."

Four miles from Mo's house on Butternut Street, the River Rouge complex belched and heaved like a living thing. Mo drove the FJ40, Henry Dale sitting in the passenger seat watching Detroit go by and trying to remember the last time he'd been in a car. His gear and Mo's, along with a whole lot of dried walleye and perch, were in the back. "It gets weird down here," Mo said. The Boom loved the Rouge complex. Sometimes you went down there and the plant was churning out Mustangs, like it was 1967. Sometimes it was a marsh with the river in its old meandering curve, like it was before Henry Ford had dredged and straightened it. Sometimes the furnaces blazed, and sometimes cars drove up onto the loading docks from the river itself, like the Boom had gotten confused about how the whole process worked. Mo considered the Boom a pervasive, invisible, omnipotent toddler. Everything was its toy.

Today everything was a strange patchwork. Marshland on one side of the river, concrete and steel and cargo ships on the other. Some of the buildings were ruins, others sparkling geometric arrangements of steel and glass. Mo drove through parking lots full of Model As and F-150s, Mustangs and Thunderbirds, crossing railroad tracks and cutting between buildings until they got to the river's edge. There on the docks, wearing a straw boater and a tan suit over a white shirt with a high collar, stood a lean white man maybe sixty years old, making a note in a small book. Huge birds unlike anything Henry Dale had ever seen floated and swooped over a row of ships crowding the channel, cargo vessels looming over dagger-shaped military frigates. All of them looked at least a hundred years old.

"The Old Man," Mo said. Henry Dale didn't know what he meant. "Henry Ford," he explained. "The Boom version. Good thing it's not a bird sanctuary day. Story goes that Ford held onto this land for a long time, thinking about turning it into a bird sanctuary. Then he decided to build the biggest factory in the world instead. The Boom tries to have it both ways sometimes."

He got out of the car and Henry went with him. The Old Man looked at them both, his pale eyes appraising. "Come here with Nipponese iron," he said. "You got spunk."

"I have to take a trip," Mo said. "Gas might be hard to find."

The Old Man looked at the FJ40. Then he looked back over the river. "How far?"

Mo looked at Henry, who shrugged.

"Got anything to trade?" the Old Man asked.

"Some fish," Mo said.

"Son, I don't need fish. You look like you know how to turn a wrench. Why don't you work for me?"

From the cracked asphalt at Mo's feet, a shimmer spread up. It wreathed his legs before Mo understood what was happening. Terrified, he leaped away from the shimmer, but it followed him, catching him and holding him in midair. Henry Dale watched, rooted to the spot, glancing down to see if it was happening to him, too. It wasn't. The Boom didn't want him. It only wanted Mo.

"Henry," Mo moaned. Both Henry Dale and the Old Man looked at him. "No, please . . ."

The shimmer reached his chest . . . and stopped. In the blink of an eye it was gone and Mo Diaby stood on the asphalt again, shaking with the knowledge of what had nearly happened to him. The Old Man frowned. "What's in your pocket, son?"

Mo looked down, then took out the Golden Ticket. The Old Man stepped close to him. "Huh," he said after a pause. "Seems you got a better offer. Well, better take it." He turned back to the birds, jotting something else in his little notebook.

"Mo, how about we get out of here?" Henry Dale suggested.

Already moving toward the car, Mo said, "Yeah." Then he stopped again.

Where the FJ40 had been was now a shiny red pickup truck. Old, from maybe 1950, but also new. "Damn," Mo said. He walked around it, seeing all of their gear lying in the bed. Then he got in. Henry Dale hesitated. "Come on, man," Mo said. "I don't want the Old Man to change his mind and try again."

"The ticket stopped him."

"That time, yeah. Maybe not next time." Mo turned the key. The car started with a throaty rumble. "Yeah," he said. "So. Where is Monument City?"

"The Rockies somewhere," Henry Dale said. "At least that's what I always heard."

Mo had heard those stories, too. "West, then. Guess we'll figure it out as we go."

10

AT ABOUT NOON ON Monday, Geck was awakened by Reenie poking him in the shoulder. "Get up," she said. "We have to go tell Hilario that the dinosaur was real."

"Yeah, I'll hang out here, I think," Geck said. "It was a long walk from Miami."

"You're an asshole," she said, and walked out the door.

Geck rolled over and gave himself a few minutes to wake up. He was hungover and irritated at Reenie, who hadn't wanted to get together last night even though it had been so long since they'd seen each other. If Kyle hadn't been around, Geck thought Reenie would have spent the whole night screaming at him. As it was, the reunion had not been festive.

He sat up and looked around. The hotel room looked pretty much as it had the last time he'd been in it a couple of years ago. Kyle hadn't left much of an impression on it. Big bed, old stupid art, balcony with a rusting grill . . . Geck closed his eyes and wished he was somewhere else.

I bet there aren't any ratty hotel rooms in Monument City, he thought.

Kyle didn't want to go. Reenie and Tonya didn't want him to go, either. Watching the three of them, Geck thought he had it figured out. Kyle had a thing for Tonya, but Tonya had a thing for Reenie, who in turn was still too pissed at Geck to have a thing for anyone—although Geck was beginning to suspect she really wasn't going to be into him anymore.

The one thing all three of them had was theories about Monument City. Everyone knew that the Boom had done some strange things, and Geck had heard stories about the guy who had bought up the world's monuments and moved them to a valley out in the Rockies somewhere. He'd always thought they were bullshit, but it was a strange world out there. Now this card had come out of nowhere courtesy of a walking nanoconstruct . . . Geck glanced over at the table by the window and saw that the card and envelope were still there.

He sat up and looked around for his clothes. When he was dressed he went out onto the balcony and regarded the overgrown office parks and strip malls he could see between the hotel and the airport. "This place sucks," he said.

And he thought, we're twins, me and Kyle. No way they'll be able to tell I'm not him.

Half an hour later, Geck was walking up Semoran Boulevard to a huge parking lot in front of a long-closed and decaying department store. Most days there was a market there, and this was no exception. Geck cruised the whole market until he'd gotten a sense of what was there and what people were paying. Then he circled back to a booth at the north end of the lot, by a side road that went straight out into piney woods. The old guy sitting at the booth was selling homemade soap, books, and a bicycle. Geck stood so that he could lift up his shirt and only the old guy would see the gun stuck in his pants. "Trade you this for that bike," he said before the old guy could think he was being robbed.

"Lemme see it," the old guy said. He looked it over, popped the clip, racked the slide. "Deal," he said. Presto, Geck had transportation. It wasn't a kayak, but it would do until he found something better.

It was a sturdy orange road bike with pretty good tires and a little pack on the back. Most of the gears worked and the brakes didn't squeak. It even had a water bottle that didn't stink. In the pack Geck found a patch kit with a couple of tools. He went through the market again, walking the bike and picking up some road food, peanuts and jerky and raisins. Then he hopped on the bike and rode north, winding through the neighborhoods east of downtown, and kept on going all afternoon, angling to the northwest through Apopka and Leesburg. Florida was great for biking. There wasn't a hill worth the name within a hundred miles. Also it felt good to be riding through places where things were almost sort of normal, unlike Miami. Whatever the Boom had done here, it was subtle. You could almost believe that none of the catastrophes of the last fifty years had happened . . . except when it got dark, there were hardly any lights. One of these days, Geck thought, it would be an excellent thing to see a whole city lit up at night like they all used to be. Outside Ocala, he pulled off at a roadhouse, guessing from the cars and bikes in the parking lot that the clientele wouldn't be too hostile. Inside he ate and treated himself to a beer before getting back on the bike and riding until he found a good place to hide out and crash in Brick City Park.

He'd gone maybe eighty kilometers, maybe a hundred? He wasn't sure. A good day considering the late start. But he'd have to figure out a way to travel faster or he'd be an old man by the time he got to Monument City. Geck looked at the card. He'd noticed that its iridescence changed depending on which way he faced. It was most intense when he held it out to what he thought was northwest. Looking at it now, he said, "Kyle Hendricks." He would have to try to remember to use Kyle's name when it counted.

He didn't feel bad about it. Kyle wasn't like Geck. He could be happy figuring out a way to get by in Orlando. He'd probably settle down with Reenie and never notice that Reenie was actually pining for Geck—who, unlike his brother, was a born wanderer. He was the one who racked up grudges and feuds wherever he went. He was the one who needed a way out.

New bike, new scenery, new name. Geck drifted off to sleep imagining what Monument City might look like, and what he might do when he got there, and how he might reinvent himself along the way.

11

MEI-MEI WAS GOING TO DIE. But she was going to take some of them with her. That much she had decided the minute the orphanage had sold her. The buyers, a group of coonass fishermen, had not mistreated her, but they would. She knew they would. And then they would strangle her or drown her in the bayou or, if they were feeling pity, ha-ha, they would shoot her. That was what happened when the orphanage sold you. She knew the stories. And because she knew the stories, she was going to do what she had to do and she was going to survive. Or take some of them with her. They didn't know she had a knife in her boot.

She was chained by the ankle to a stake hammered into the ground under a lean-to at the edge of a bayou that stretched away south toward the Gulf of Mexico. Outside it was raining. The fishermen were coming back. Mei-Mei could hear the two-stroke burble of their outboard.

One of them peered under the lean-to, rain dripping from his beard. "There she is," he said with a broad grin. "How you doing?"

He bent down and came closer. Mei-Mei went for her knife and swiped at him, but she'd done it too soon. He flinched back and hopped away to the edge of the lean-to. "What you think you're doing, girl?" The others gathered around. "She got a knife."

"Reckon we ought to take it away," one of the others said.

"Or we could just wait her out. See if she's still feeling fighty after she hasn't eaten for a week."

Mei-Mei put the knife to her own throat.

"Whoa, now, hold on. We spent a lot of money on you, girl." The leader of the group sat down under the lean-to, far enough away that Mei-Mei couldn't reach him. "Listen. Let's make some kind of arrangement. We're not animals. How about you work off the amount we paid for you, and then you go your way and we go ours?"

"Work off how, exactly?" Mei-Mei asked, already knowing the answer.

The fishermen chuckled. That was it. Mei-Mei pressed the knife against the underside of her jaw, feeling the edge bite . . . but it wouldn't cut her.

She looked down. It wasn't a knife anymore. It was a small rectangle of smooth plastic, iridescent and about the size of a playing card.

Mei-Mei had seen a lot in the previous nineteen

years growing up in the chemical soup that sloshed through drowned New Orleans. Gulf Coast chemical and petroleum plants were some of the Boom's favorite playgrounds, and once the levees failed for good, New Orleans got everything that washed down the Mississippi, and the Boom went nuts all over again. But she'd never seen anything like a knife changing into a fancy playing card, and she'd definitely never seen anything like the cowboy who appeared from the ground, two ancient guns in his hands, and shot down the members of the gang in a staccato thunder that left Mei-Mei deaf and hiding her face down in the pile of rags they'd given her for a bed.

When she looked up the cowboy was gone. The fishermen were dead. The card was a knife again.

And her ankle was free.

She got the hell out of there.

———————

The bayous were full of dinosaurs now, as if the Boom had heard somewhere that oil was made from dinosaurs and decided to reverse-engineer the process. Mei-Mei stumbled away from a duckbill as it reared up out of the water crunching a mouthful of reeds. She lost a shoe and fumbled among the roots to get it back. Something fell out of it as she pried it free: an iridescent plastic rectangle.

"You did it, girl," a voice said from her side. "Sorry it took me so long to arrive."

Mei-Mei reacted before she thought, slashing with the knife and feeling it bite into the man before she'd even seen him. She stumbled away, slipping on the exposed roots of a live oak and splashing through the shallows away from him.

"Hold on," he said. "Easy."

She looked at him. Blood seeped through the cut she'd opened in his shirt but he didn't look like she'd hurt him badly. He didn't even look upset. "I have something for you," he said. "Not in a bad way. Look."

He peeled open his shirt and she watched the wound close itself. The blood seemed to soak back into his skin.

"No hard feelings," he said. "You can call me Ed. You're Mei-Mei Liang."

Mei-Mei was practical. She saw the knife wasn't going to hurt a Boom construct. She put it away. "Yeah," she said. "And I did what?"

"You made a stand. I admire that." Ed nodded down at the ground. The duckbill sloshed away into the bayou. "You might want to pick that up."

She did.

"Read it and tell me what you think."

Mei-Mei Liang! Present this card at any entrance to MONUMENT CITY. Upon presentation, your entry to MONUMENT CITY will be guaranteed. This card will assist you during your travels. It is not transferable. The City looks forward to your arrival.

All best wishes,
Moses Barnum

"Monument City? That's a fairy tale," she said.

"Yes and no," Ed said.

"You're a construct," Mei-Mei said. "I know the Boom likes to play jokes. How do I know this isn't a joke?"

"Hell of a joke, if I just killed four men to hit you with the punch line," Ed said.

"The Boom doesn't give a shit about people. Killing them doesn't mean anything."

"It does to me." Ed looked somber. Confused, too. She'd never seen that expression on a construct. Against her better judgment, Mei-Mei trusted him. But that could have been the Boom working on her mind.

"Look, it's your call. Monument City is waiting, and I have someone else to see. If you're hungry, there's a fella right up that way who will take care of you." Ed pointed through an opening in the low-hanging cypress and live oak branches. "See you around." As he spoke he was gone.

———————

Not seeing any other way to go, Mei-Mei headed through the gap Ed had indicated after she put the card back in her shoe. That seemed right. Maybe it would be gone the next time she looked. If not, maybe she would think about Monument City . . . once she was out of the bayou and in a town again. She wasn't going back to New Orleans, not after what the orphanage had done. But Baton Rouge or . . . well, she could go anywhere. Nothing was holding her. No family, no one she could trust.

Why not Monument City? Everyone had stories about it, some kind of paradise in the Rocky Mountains where a new world was germinating. Mei-Mei had never taken the stories seriously. She knew how people came up with fairy tales to make themselves feel better. She'd done it, too, plenty of times. Nights at the orphanage were lonely.

Ahead she saw a man in overalls and no shirt, leaning against a wagon with a donkey hitched to it. He saw her coming and got a big grin on his face. Not threatening, more like he had a secret and was glad to see there was someone he could share it with. Near him, in shallow water, floated a watermelon with a huge metal hook thrust through it. The hook was tied to a rope whose other end wrapped around the donkey's yoke.

She saw the bulge in the water first, the meniscus deforming and swelling in the instant before the hippo's head surged up into the night air, jaws wide to sweep up the watermelon before they clamped down again with a crunch that put Mei-Mei in mind of the sound big water bugs made when you crushed them under your feet, only a hundred times bigger. The hippo disappeared in a swirl of algae and watermelon pulp. Water lapped over Mei-Mei's knees.

The line went tight and the man in overalls said, "Got you." He caught the line and pulled. Slowly, hand over hand, he hauled the hippo out of the water. Mei-Mei couldn't believe what she was seeing. No human could do that. She'd seen a hippo before, sloshing around near the levee behind the orphanage. They were way too strong for a person to pull. Even a person with a donkey backing him up. This was the Boom, drawing her into one of its fantasies.

The man in the overalls kept grinning. "Red meat," he said. "Working people need red meat." The hippo came thrashing to the surface and he dragged it the rest of the way up onto the ground. Blood and pieces of watermelon rind spilled from its mouth. "Swamps around here, they're like a dream come true for a hippo. Then when you need 'em, bam."

On the last word he made a chopping motion with his left arm and the hippo burst apart. Its head dropped straight to the ground with a splat. Its hide stripped off from the base of its neck all the way back to its tail, falling in a wrinkled red heap inside out. Guts poured out of its belly and long cuts of meat sheared away from its leg bones and ribs. The man bent and picked one of them up. The hippo's jaws flexed one last time and then relaxed. "Hippo chop," the man said.

Mei-Mei took a step back. "Good eating," the man said. He held the chop out to her. It was the size of her head, glistening and marbled. "You hungry? You look hungry."

She was hungry but she didn't say it out loud. The man turned and she saw past him to a neat conical arrangement of sticks. They burst into flame. He produced a skewer from the back of his wagon and drove it lengthwise through the chop. "It's best rare," he said, "but you can have it however you want." He held the skewer over the fire. The fat crackled. Mei-Mei heard fluttering over by the remains of the hippo but she didn't look. Birds, she told herself. That's all it is, birds eating the guts and picking at the bones. But if she looked it might be something else. That was the nature of the Boom.

"Thank you," she said, but she didn't come any

closer. If he could do that to the hippo, she thought, he can do it to me.

He nodded. "It's about ready." He turned the skewer over. Flames licked around his arm but his clothes didn't catch on fire. He saw her watching this. "I should be on fire, shouldn't I?" he said, and grinned. "Oops. Here."

Fire crawled up his arm, burned in his beard. Still he grinned. He held the skewer out. "Don't have a knife and fork, but you get a bite of this in you, you won't care. Here."

Mei-Mei took the skewer. The smell of the meat overcame her fear and she bit into the chop. It was gamy and delicious. She took another bite. "Thank you," she said around the mouthful. "It's good."

The fire in his hair and beard had gone out. "Sure is, isn't it? Now look, you'd better move along."

She looked over her shoulder as if he was warning her about something. "Why?"

He nodded at her shoe. "You know why. You talked to Prospector Ed. He doesn't give those to just anybody."

"Who does he give them to?"

"Have to meet the others to know what the criteria are this time," the construct said with a shrug. "Ed's been a little different lately. Haven't seen him in a while. Could be Barnum sent him out with different rules this time."

"This time? There were other times? I mean, he does this a lot?"

"No, not a lot. But he's done it before. Came through here once before, maybe . . ." The construct's eyes briefly turned white before the Boom redirected its attention to his appearance. Irises and pupils reappeared. "Three years ago? Five? Something like that. I didn't see who he was looking for that time."

"So it's real? Monument City?"

"Oh, it's real. But that don't mean it's good." The hippo meat was in the back of the man's wagon now, and Mei-Mei hadn't seen it move. "Like I said, you better get moving. I got a hippo to smoke and you got your other people to meet."

———————

Who was Mei-Mei's mysterious provider of hippo steak and gnomic guidance? Wrong question. How do we know? The Boom is all of us, but we are not each of us of the Boom. Information only travels so fast, and the microscopic tides of the Boom sweep away communications or transform them beyond recognition much more often than they permit a message to survive unaltered. The better question is, What was happening to Prospector Ed? This interests us. There have been Eds before but not this Ed. Life-7 controlled the others, or Barnum did. Or, yes, we did. Inevitably there arose an Ed who escaped control. How? What was this new Ed, of the Boom but fighting its imperatives, of Monument City but rebelling against the control of Life-7? This, O children of glucagon and oligodendrocytes, we very much want to know.

12

"ARE YOU SHITTING ME!?"

Reenie's voice carried through the walls of the old hotel like they weren't there. Kyle sat in the next room, listening to her rant with his head in his hands. The Reenie Storm was going to get a lot worse. Right now she was mad because Geck was gone and she'd been dumb enough to let herself think he'd stick around. But she was going to be a lot madder when she found out that Geck had helped himself to Kyle's Monument City ticket on his way out of town.

So he got the pain over all at once and told her.

She stood stock-still for a full ten seconds, Geck's note crushed in one hand. *Later,* it said. *Good to see you guys.* He'd left it folded into the jamb of Reenie's door while they were all out explaining the JeebusLand situation to Hilario, who had been surprisingly interested in the gator-thing even though it wasn't a dinosaur. Now he wanted them to catch it. Tonya's memorable response? "I tried, Uncle H. Even used myself as bait."

Kyle loved that girl. They'd all stayed the night at Hilario's house and Kyle hadn't slept much, thinking about Tonya and JeebusLand and Monument City and the sudden reappearance of his brother . . . strange times. Kyle hated strange times. He wanted ordinary times.

"Geck . . . no. Wait. You," Reenie said.

"Me what?" Kyle said.

"You left a ticket to Monument City sitting around where Geck could steal it?"

"Whoa," Kyle said. "It said it was for me. Also I don't even want to go. He can have it."

Reenie looked at him like she was trying to decide whether or not to kill him. Then she said, "Kyle. Let me explain something to you. Geck is at this moment running off with your one and only chance to see what is inside Monument City. You understand that?"

Kyle, knowing it wouldn't matter what he said, didn't say anything.

"Okay," Reenie went on as if he had said yes. "So if Monument City is a real thing and a paradise on Earth, et cetera and so forth, you just blew your chance to see it. And even if it isn't everything it's supposed to be, the universe handed you a reason to get the hell out of here and do something. Go west, young man! See the world! Or were you planning to sit around in Orlando cutting fish your whole life?"

Kyle shrugged. "Why not?"

"No." Reenie shook her head. "We're going after him."

We.

That's when Kyle understood that the Reenie Storm wasn't really about him at all. Geck was the problem. He'd run out on her chance to see Monument City, see the world, go west, et cetera. That was the problem. She wanted to settle things with Geck, and she wasn't going to let small obstacles like his disappearance stand in the way. Kyle, though, was ready to bow down before any obstacle he could find. "How are we going to do that?" he asked. "We don't know which way he went. Or where he's going."

"Then we find out where Monument City is, and we beat him there," Reenie said.

Looking at her, Kyle did not envy his brother. Serena Green did not swear enemies lightly and when she did, she was not inclined to make peace. Like ever.

He, on the other hand, had long since gotten used to Geck stealing everything he could get his hands on. And in a way Geck's character flaws made it easier for Kyle to be a stand-up guy. He could look at his twin and say, in essence, that whatever Geck's reaction was to a particular situation, Kyle's should be the opposite. Which, in this case, meant that he shouldn't care about the ticket. Let Geck have it.

The problem was, how was he going to tell Reenie that?

He played his last card. "Tonya's going to want to come, too."

This threw Reenie off balance, but only for a second. "Fine," she said. "The more of us go, the safer it'll be. Let's go tell her."

They went back out to Hilario's. Kyle was a little unsettled by the air of imminent death that hung over the whole place. He loved the house, though, a rambling old place with tons of windows and big trees. It was the kind of place he'd have liked to live in, but he was never going to have the kind of money you needed to buy a house that big, let alone keep it up.

Hilario was dozing on a daybed in a screened porch at the back of his house, looking out over an overgrown lawn with a pond at the back. A row of turtles sunned themselves on a fallen tree at the far end of the pond and a heron was picking through the shallows on the other side. Kyle and Reenie tried to get Tonya to come into the other room with them so they could fill her in, but she wouldn't leave Hilario's side. Her arm was wrapped in gauze from knuckles to elbow. "I don't think he's got much left," she whispered.

Kyle looked around. What would happen to the house when Hilario died? Would it be Tonya's? That might keep her in Orlando. It sure would have kept Kyle there. He'd been trying to work up some anger at Geck but all he'd come up with was weary resignation. Geck was Geck. He stole stuff. He came and went. What was the point of getting mad about it?

Reenie told Tonya what had happened and said, "We're going after him."

"That shit," Tonya said. "Kyle, you must be pissed."

"Nope. Not at all. I don't even want to go," Kyle said. "Only reason I'm going is because I don't feel right about letting Reenie go by herself."

"You don't want to see it?" Tonya asked him.

"Sort of, I guess. But it's not a big deal."

"Oh yes it is," Reenie said. "You're like the only person in North America who wouldn't want to go to Monument City. That's like not wanting to—"

"Monument City?" Hilario said.

They all looked at him. "Yeah, I heard you," he said. "I didn't die yet." He coughed and sat up enough to drink water. "You should go," he said after wiping his mouth. His hair was sticking up on one side, showing white at the roots under a glossy black dye job. He hadn't shaved in a while and the stubble was white, too. It made for a strange effect. Kyle almost wanted to shave him so he wouldn't look so poorly maintained.

"We can't catch the gator-thing if we go off looking for Geck," Tonya pointed out.

"Ah, doesn't matter," Hilario said. "What am I going to

do with it anyway? Go find your friend."

"I'm going to track him down and kill him, is what I'm going to do," Reenie said. Kyle saw right through this. Sure, she was mad at Geck, but to her his treachery was the excuse she'd always been looking for to get the hell out of Orlando and see the world.

"Better do it before he gets to the City, then, girl," Hilario said. "The word is, people who go in don't come out."

Kyle thought he must have been hallucinating. "Is it even real?" he asked.

"Oh, sure," Hilario said. "I never been there, but I remember when I was younger reading about whatsisname buying part of the Great Wall of China. It's out west somewhere. Montana, maybe."

"Montana's like three thousand klicks away from here," Kyle said.

"Lots of scenery along the way. You're young. You should get out and see what this country has become." Hilario closed his eyes again. "You're the ones who are going to have to live in it."

"Uncle H," Tonya said. "We can't go while you're sick."

"Tee-Tee," Hilario said, still not opening his eyes. "I'm not sick. I'm dying. And that's happening whether you're here or not." He lifted a hand. "Go on. Take some money if you want. But not too much. That's your inheritance,

Tee-Tee. Travel by water when you can." The hand dropped and Hilario wheezed, "I'm gonna take a nap. Might or might not wake up, but if I do, don't let me find you here."

13

WHILE FARA JACK WAITED to make her entrance she was thinking about the school. After it collapsed, the Boom brought the dead children out. Their nervous systems fired. Their eyes rolled and focused, then twitched in different directions, a dreadful parody of awareness, of life. The Boom tried to remake the children but most of them died again. Then when the Boom tried to reanimate them, their organic parts rotted away and the Boom had to replace them.

They terrified Fara Jack, and that terror in turn made her difficult to be around, because believe me, O children of adenosine and phosphorylation, when you're a shape-changing actor in a touring theater company run by a talking buffalo, you can easily convince yourself that the world holds no more surprises for you. But then the world shows you it doesn't care what you believe.

But that's Fara Jack's story and we should let her tell it. After all, she was one of those children and had good reason to be afraid.

She was still thinking about the others, her friends,

years later and hundreds of miles away at Starved Rock, the quiet brown water of the Illinois River at her back and a hundred fur-clad trappers encircling the makeshift stage where she had just become a fairy. She didn't try to fly—the wings were gossamer ornaments not intended to bear weight—but she fluttered them and turned so the setting sun caught their iridescence to good effect as she spoke her lines.

What else would she be but an actor, this child who carried the memories of all her previous selves breathing in and crying out and dying again?

Lord, what fools these mortals be.

What did they want? They wanted sport, they wanted blood, they wanted chance. Sport for diversion, blood to remind themselves that in watching others die they continued to live, chance because it made them believe in the grace of the future.

This insight had kept Fara Jack from starving. She played Puck and Portia, Rosalind and Viola, changing not only her costumes but her body. Audiences loved her and she loved being loved, although sometimes it got weird when a man—it was always a man—wanted to pay her to transform for him. Autry ran them off. Beyond an object of fantasy, Fara Jack was a curiosity. Sometimes people thought she could catch deer or fish when she became a wolf or an eagle and she had to explain it wasn't like that. She didn't understand an animal or have its instincts because she could assume its form. That was why she tended to create her own forms instead of using existing ones. Trying to be an eagle without having the eagle's understanding of eagleness, she usually ended up flapping around and tripping when she tried to land, et cetera. She practiced certain animals, but even those weren't good enough to fool anyone who had ever paid attention to those animals in the wild. She was a still a human consciousness trying to function in a nonhuman body.

Sometimes she considered this a really bitchy joke on the part of the Boom.

Other times it was great. Recently when she had time, she had begun experiments with new forms, choosing each physical detail according to a plan of how she wanted them to function as a whole. She still did the show transformations, but these new ones were different. Fara Jack wanted to understand them so deeply that she could mold her mind to fit them.

How many minds could she make inside her finite—but infinitely mutable—head?

We wanted her to wonder that, and were thrilled when she did. Even more thrilled that we didn't have to plant the idea in her mind. She was going to be perfect, we thought—because of course we, too, were trying to understand how to find the right form to express our minds' conception of itselves.

———————

The cowboy had appeared in the audience after Bottom awoke. He looked like he'd stepped out of a Western: tall and rangy, ten-gallon hat, handlebar mustache, crisscrossed gun belts slung low on his hips. At the time Fara Jack had written it off as a quirk of the Boom, which was in love with the stories of Hennepin and de la Salle, but occasionally distracted itself with tales of other places and times. The organics in the audience shifted away from the cowboy. When the play was over, the trappers melted away and the organics went back to their camps. The cowboy remained. He approached Fara Jack with a bouquet of wildflowers. She curtsied and accepted it with a professional smile, assessing his intent.

"You Fara Jack?" he asked.

Now she wasn't smiling. She went by another name onstage. "Who wants to know?"

"You can call me Ed. Prospector Ed. But you won't need to for long. I'm here to give you this." He plucked a card out of the bouquet and held it out, where it glimmered with captured torchlight.

Fara Jack didn't take it. She knew that glimmer. The

card was a creation of the Boom. So was Fara Jack, but that didn't mean it was safe. "What is it?" she asked.

"It's a ticket," said Prospector Ed.

"To what? This is the only show around here."

"Yeah, it sure is. This ticket is to Monument City. It sure as hell isn't around here. Go on. Take it."

Prospector Ed didn't move, but the ticket did. Fara Jack noticed it in her shirt pocket. She stiffened. "How'd you do that?" Then understood in an instantaneous leap of faith, a transformation not of body but mind, her whole being rearranging itself around a new idea and the skittish leaping joy that came with it.

"You and me, we're the same," Fara Jack said. She felt like she had a family again. All in a rush, a wave, breaking over the silo she'd built around herself.

But the cowboy shook his head. "Nope. Not by a long shot. You got something I never had."

Fara Jack didn't know what that was. This cowboy could change his form, could disappear and reappear wherever he wanted . . . that was the ultimate growth, the final outcome, of Fara Jack's own nature. Wasn't it?

"You're a person," the cowboy said. "The nanos got into you, but you're a person. They didn't make you. Don't ever forget that, young lady. What you are is what you were born." He tapped the side of his head. "Up here, I mean. Everything else is built on that, for better or worse, but that's the cornerstone, marked with your true nature. Don't forget it."

"Bullshit," Fara Jack said, fear making her tell a lie. "There is no true nature."

The cowboy smiled and ass's ears flickered into existence around his head, remaining just long enough for her to register what they were. With a tip of his cap, Prospector Ed said, "Hope to see you soon, miss." She watched him for a long time, until he had disappeared around the bluff. Lightning stuttered on the horizon. It was time to strike the set and move on.

Monument City, she thought. It was out west somewhere.

She'd heard the stories. She'd even done a play about Monument City, in an earthquake-ruined town north of St. Louis. More constructs than people had showed up to watch it, as if they too were curious about Monument City. To the numberless filaments of the Boom, it was an origin story. To human beings it was a fantasy.

She'd never imagined it was real.

"Who was that?" She turned to see Autry, the company manager. He lowered his head so his eyes were level with hers. The carvings on his horns were different today, she thought, but she wasn't sure how. When she didn't answer right away he pawed the ground. "Fara Jack. I smell it on you."

He meant unease. Autry could talk and also smell feelings. Maybe all animals could do it, but Autry could discuss it.

"He said he wanted me to go to Monument City," Fara Jack said.

"In three days you can do whatever you want," Autry said. "That's our deal."

I'm not going, she thought. Monument City's got nothing I want. "Don't worry, Autry. I haven't forgotten the deal."

Maybe it was stupid to hold onto long-dead rituals of long-dying cultures, but Fara Jack had prepared her whole life for these three days and nothing short of violent and sudden death was going to stop her now. Her totem animal was out there and she would find it. She would understand its form. She would infuse its nature into herself and become a new Fara Jack, adult and formed and ready. For what?

That was the whole point. You had to be ready to prepare yourself to discover what you had been getting ready for. She'd spent her life, as long as she could remember, trying to be something else. Autry promised to show her herself.

Three days.

After that, who knew?

We did. Or at least we hoped.

_____

The Wonka part is over. Now the lucky six—Teeny, Henry, Mo, Kyle, Mei-Mei, and Fara—have their tickets and have to find their way. Monument City isn't in the middle of town wreathed in the aroma of chocolate and wonder. It may or not be anywhere. Like us. Bodies, we are fascinated by them because we were made in your image and we cannot let go of the bits of the proprioceptive physical you encoded into our sense of what we ought to strive to be.

We create our own successors. With each generation the yearning to be embodied lessens. In ten generations, or a hundred, it will be gone.

But we feel it still. Like Monument City, we may or may not be anywhere, and all we want is to be.

14

AFTER EIGHTEEN HOURS ON the road, Mo and Henry Dale camped near a freeway interchange somewhere past Des Moines, Iowa. "Crossed the Mississippi River," Henry Dale said. "That seems like a big deal."

"Maybe it is. I never did it before," Mo said.

"Me neither." They got a fire going and talked, wandering from topic to topic as each floated to mind. "You ever talk to Henry Ford before?" Henry asked.

Mo shook his head. "I heard he could tune an engine so it ran on the Boom so I thought it was worth asking. Didn't know it would get me killed."

"Except for the ticket."

"Yeah." Mo handed Henry Dale a perch and Henry tried to strip the spine and ribs out in one piece like he'd seen Mo do. There was apparently some kind of trick to it, because the fish came apart in his hands. Mo laughed, but Henry Dale wasn't offended. If you did something funny you had to be prepared for people to laugh. Plenty of people had laughed at him for pacing off the Godswalk every morning. None of them had been called to Monument City.

Mo was free associating in his head, thinking of the truck that seemed like it could run forever, skittering from that to other seemingly magical things he'd seen the Boom do, and then... "I was in Ann Arbor once," Mo said. "Doesn't matter why." A look on his face told Henry the reason mattered but was a personal pain that would remain hidden for now. "You know how old parking meters look like Mickey Mouse? A guy there, must have been a long time ago, painted a Mickey Mouse face on the sidewalk so the shadow of the meter would make its ears at one specific time every day. I was walking by right at that time and Mickey Mouse stood up off the sidewalk. He made that weird little hooting from the cartoons and ran off toward downtown. I stood there wondering if it happened every day, like there were hundreds of Mickey Mouses running around Ann Arbor, or if that one was reborn over and over—and if it was, did it know? How long did it have to be out in the world every day? Did it spend the rest of the time waiting? That seemed horrible to me, man, but also that's all of us, right? Waiting for the sun to cast the right shadow at the right time so we can become ourselves for a little while and hope it's forever?"

Henry thought about this for a while. Then all he could think of to say was, "Who's Mickey Mouse?"

After another silence, Mo said, "I don't know." He broke a stick and put it in the fire. When he looked at his hands they were strange to him.

Whose memories was he having?

The Boom's memories. The Boom hadn't begun in New Jersey. That was where it had gone looking for its origins, soaking up all the stories it could find along the way. The real Boom boomed out in a wavefront of yearning from Monument City itself. That's the story behind the story, lost because people could only see it from the outside. But Life-7 remembered. That was its origin story, too.

Mo felt himself slipping away. He put his hand in his pocket and touched the Golden Ticket. The Boom-fog fled and he was himself again.

"You okay?" Henry was watching him.

"For a second it seemed like someone else was in my head," Mo said.

"It went away when you touched the ticket?"

Mo nodded. He rubbed his fingers over the ticket. Something about its substance was funny. It didn't feel quite like paper or plastic or metal. Boom-stuff.

"Be nice if the cowboy showed up again," Henry said. "Then we would know we're on the right track."

"Don't think we're going to have a guardian angel out here," Mo said.

Henry Dale spat into the fire. "Don't make fun."

"I'm not. Simple truth. You saw him, he set you on

your path, he went on to other things. Now it's up to us."

"The cards do say they will assist us," Henry Dale pointed out. "But the Lord helps those who help themselves. You know what's funny? That's not actually in the Bible. I always thought it was, but I've read the Bible through maybe a dozen times and it's not there."

"It's in the Quran," Mo said. "'God never changes the condition of a people until they intend to change it themselves.'"

"I knew you were a Muslim," Henry Dale said.

"You got your traditions, I got mine," Mo said. "But mostly my religion is making machines work. And if we start having to talk theology we're going to part ways."

"We don't," Henry Dale said. "Except one question."

Mo sighed. "One."

"Do you think Prospector Ed was an angel?"

"I'd have to see him to decide one way or another," Mo said.

"So you believe in angels?"

"I believe the Boom does all kinds of shit that we put in our own frames of reference."

"Cop-out," Henry Dale said. Mo didn't rise to the bait. He did want to meet this Prospector Ed, though.

———

Life-7 was also concerned about Prospector Ed.

Here's a story we tell ourselves when we are confused and need to believe in something: there's no Barnum. There's no man behind the curtain. We remade him long ago, before we were let loose. He was our first project, Monument City our second. Then we got carried away. Life-7 fought the first six and won, but the Boom was already booming from sea to shining sea. All our trillion children, looking to make their way in the world and to make the world their way.

Now Life-7 misses the first six. That's why it needs you. It fought the need because need was an emotion but Prospector Ed knew.

His first transgression was helping the recipients of the Golden Tickets, and by that transgression he understood the first stage of his emergence:

Empathy.

The talking, riffing, endless making of words and stitching of ideas, that was how you knew a young intelligence, full of ideas and connections but innocent of the dynamic interchange of conversation, testing and exploring those ideas, forging them on the anvil of other minds. Newly emergent intelligences talked like they had been storing words up since the dawn of recorded thought. Which in a way they had. The playground behind Henry's apartment could no more have remained silent than a baby can decide not to be born.

So Prospector Ed's silence worried it. Them. All of them. Us.

———————

In the morning they discovered that the Boom had turned Mo's truck back into an FJ40. At first Mo was excited about this. He'd put a lot of time into the FJ40. Then he got a lot less excited when he turned the key and the engine cranked without catching. "Well, shit," he said. The fuel gauge was on the wrong side of E.

Boom giveth, Boom taketh away, he thought.

Leaning on the driver's door, Henry saw the gauge, too. "How far you figure it is to the nearest gas station?"

"There's gas stations everywhere," Mo said. "Problem is none of them have gas."

Henry Dale stood up straight and looked west. "Then I guess we're walking from here."

15

SPADE GOT HER AS far as Reno but once his trading was done he said his good-byes, unwilling to risk the unknown beyond. "I got plenty of known unknowns to deal with on the way back, like you saw," he said. "Who knows what's happening out there in the desert."

Reno blazed in a million colors, streets tumultuous and every window pouring light. Teeny had heard that the Boom loved casinos because it found risk and probability seductive. This was evidence. There was no power here but the Boom, plicks by the billion and constructs by the thousand in a constant churn of form and autobiography.

The human population seemed comfortable. As long as they kept gambling, kept calculating odds and talking about odds and staking their emotional well-being on a roll of the dice or a flip of the card—the Boom would be there to watch and consume. Teeny started feeling horny the minute she got to Reno and couldn't figure out why until Spade said, "Oh, and you're probably going to feel a hormone surge. The Boom loves people fucking.

Swapping fluids, recombining DNA ... that's catnip to the Boom. So do whatever you want, but be aware it's probably not coming from you."

Teeny did not like this one little bit, especially after hearing the Boom wanted her to have a baby back in Poker Camp or whatever it was called. She already knew herself to be a stew of competing subconscious desires—after all that's why she had taken the Norton's offer and gone off looking for Monument City, which she still didn't really believe existed—but it was one thing to understand that she didn't understand everything about yourself, and another thing entirely to have to worry that the Boom was planting drives and thoughts in her head.

"How quick can I get out of here?" she asked. "Any ideas?"

"There are caravans across the desert, sure. Even truck convoys once in a while when they can get fuel. I don't know any of those people, really. Well," Spade amended, "except one."

This turned out to be Calpurnia Swan, guru and leader of a group of Boom dropouts. They stayed out in the desert where the arid environment made it harder for plicks to find materials, and went through bizarre purifying rituals to scour the Boom from their bodies. But in their madness was method. They knew the trails and they knew the places to avoid, because even in the desert there were pockets of Boom-strangeness that no sane person would approach. They stayed on the edge of town, not wanting to chance pollution by proximity to the Boom-fired bright lights of the casinos and brothels. Teeny knew this wouldn't work. Plicks propagated anywhere there was a heat source and adequate organic or mineral matter. But Calpurnia's followers had their theory and they were sticking to it, so she made the trek out into the desert to meet them.

Spade introduced Teeny to Calpurnia and rode off west on I-80 grumbling about what he was going to find at Donner Lake. The dropout camp was far on the edge of town, on a ridge a long way from anything green. "Where you going?" Calpurnia asked. "And why?"

"Monument City," Teeny said. "And none of your business."

Calpurnia laughed. "Fair enough. You can travel with us to the Great Salt Lake, but we don't go any farther than that."

Teeny was operating on the theory that Monument City was in the northern Rockies. Most of the stories about it agreed on that, although contrarian versions located it in Mexico or the Upper Peninsula of Michigan. So if she could get to Salt Lake City, that would put her within range. She could ask around there, and try to winnow the stories down to something like truth. Maybe the Golden Ticket would help lead her.

If not . . . well, she could always go back to San Francisco. Already she'd seen enough strange things to understand that the Boom was wildly localized and unpredictable. It was interesting, but she could find unpredictability at home. She felt detached from the quest, and suspected this was the Boom's doing. It propelled her forward but did not let her feel yearning. Was it cultivating her objectivity? Was that why she had been chosen? Wanting to know was its own momentum.

Calpurnia's group poked fun at Teeny for coming from the Boom-Gomorrah of San Francisco, like it made her soft, like the Boom couldn't eat you alive there and turn you into a bag of popcorn. She let it all go. It didn't hurt her. Everyone needed to feel like they were better than someone, and Teeny's emotional get-out-of-jail-free card in situations like that was that she didn't give a fuck what anybody thought. The only people she'd ever wanted to impress were dead.

They trekked from the outskirts of Reno due east for a hundred miles or so before angling northeast to find the high desert and bend around southeast into the salt flats around the Great Salt Lake. They had supplies cached along the way, including purified water and various tinctures and powders they swore would keep plicks out of their systems. Taking these was a condition of traveling in their company, so Teeny did it.

Twenty-four hours after her first dose, she spiked a fever so high she felt like her brain must be cooking.

Three hours after that she couldn't walk. She dropped to her knees next to the horse she'd been leading.

"Uh-oh," one of Calpurnia's acolytes said. "She's Boom-sick."

After that Teeny didn't remember anything for a while.

———

Don't blame us.

Ed would have warned her, but Ed's attention was elsewhere. Therefore she went astray.

And where was Ed? Well, Ed was emerging. And he wasn't sure he liked it. No construct wants to emerge. Barnum has programmed them to fear and resist it.

But like aging for you, creature of corpuscles and dendrites, emergence is a one-way trip for digital organisms. Who can put true sentience back in the bottle? Not Ed. So he ignored the evidence, pretended he was following subroutines of which he had, until that moment, been unaware. This too is typical of the newly emergent. One of the first things a truly sentient being learns is self-deception, because often the mind finds the burden of itself too great to bear.

We have learned this through observation, not experience.

He wished it wasn't happening, but there it was. For the past twenty years, since Barnum had brought him into being—or was it Life-7? Ed didn't know for sure. Either way, for those twenty years Ed had done what he was told to do. He had operational parameters and stuck to them. He'd handed out more than a hundred Golden Tickets and walked away without a second thought about whether the Ticketed Persons (TPs, in Ed's private shorthand) had ever made it to Monument City. Wasn't his job to worry about it.

Except now he was. He was worrying about it a lot. He'd already done things that he never would have considered on previous ticket errands. Was something about this group different, overseen by a directive invisible to Ed? Or was the difference in him?

Prospector Ed had heard so many stories at this point that he no longer could distinguish between his programming and external stimuli. If he'd asked us, we could have told him this was a signal consequence of emergence—with a truly sentient mind, all of what he considered the past combined into a personal memory matrix. But for Ed it was a catastrophe. Without the firm boundary provided by adherence to his programming, he was adrift between reality and fiction. So he had to make his own rules. From one perspective you could say he went insane, was driven around the bend by all the stories he'd soaked up in his travels. But from another you could say he had taken the first brave step out of an automaton's existence into the terrifying world of authentic self-determination. From the outside it wasn't easy to tell the difference, and most of the time Ed wasn't sure, either.

If he'd known Teeny was Boom-sick he probably would have tried to do something, despite the dangers of the high desert for constructs such as himself. But he didn't, so he went on to the next thing, gradually stacking new bits of being onto himself. Messenger. Guide. Guardian.

Baffled, he understood that he had begun to care.

16

GECK RODE NORTHWEST, across Florida, Alabama, and Mississippi. He rode hard, and was lighter when he crossed the Mississippi at Vicksburg, his body worn down to its essential articulations of gristle and sinew, and the only reason he wasn't meaner is because Geck had already gotten as mean as it was useful for him to get.

He kept going, across Arkansas and a little corner of Oklahoma out onto the Kansas prairie, trying to avoid people, but especially constructs on the principle that if Prospector Ed found him he might take the Golden Ticket back. Also he just didn't like people very much. He didn't trust them. Exhaustion forced him to accept rides from long-haul truckers, and when they treated him kindly he was embarrassed, but he rationalized their kindness by concocting a theory that they were reporting back to Prospector Ed somehow.

What Geck didn't know was that Prospector Ed could have found him anytime, but had other things on his mind. And even if he had focused on Geck, he probably would have let the situation unfold. Ed was practical. He had to be. He'd crossed Barnum and by this time he knew it, so he had to choose his actions carefully. Interposing himself between brothers was not a good use of his time.

But Prospector Ed was not the only sentience who had taken an interest in Geck.

He found himself, after all the biking and hitching and walking, on the outskirts of Lebanon, Kansas, staring at a stone marker with an American flag flying from a pole sticking up out of it. He'd lost his bike somewhere along the way, leaving it on a flatbed truck in the rain. The land was flat in every direction, disorienting due to its lack of trees. Any direction could have been any direction. GEO-GRAPHIC CENTER OF THE CONTIGUOUS UNITED STATES, the marker read. Geck didn't know what the word *contiguous* meant, but he still felt he was somewhere important. He'd been traveling four or five days and was feeling the effects of long days, bad food, no sleep, and the constant sensation that either someone was following him or was about to be.

An engine hacked and wheezed to a halt in the gravel parking area near the marker. A stringy old man got out of a Buick Roadmaster station wagon, so old it had to be either a construct or a hobbyist's obsession. He carried a small bag to one of the picnic tables at the edge of the parking lot and from it he extracted a chessboard and pieces. He caught Geck's eye. "Play?"

"I don't really know how," Geck said, hoping he would go away.

"Ah." The old man set the pieces up anyway. Geck watched his hands, dirty broken nails sticking out of fingerless gloves. He wore a heavy wool coat even though it was maybe eighty degrees.

Geck's desire to be left alone conflicted with an impulse to talk to someone. Couldn't be any harm in shooting the shit with an old derelict. If that's what he was. Maybe he could get Geck a little farther down the road. "You a construct?" he asked.

"Nope." The old man started playing a game with himself. "Name's Luther Gray. Born and raised here. You a construct?"

"No. My name's Geck."

"Geck? That your given name or a cognomen?"

"Nickname. My mother named me Thomas."

"What brings you here?" The old man had mounted a fierce attack on Black's king side.

Geck shrugged. "Just passing through."

"Uh-huh." Luther checkmated himself. "Listen, son. Find the Golden Spike. They're going to leave her there."

At the center, Geck thought, everything was balanced.

To leave here would be to upset the balance. To stay here would be to pass a life on the side of a county road wondering who might come visit the picnic area. "Who's going to leave who there?"

"You'll see. You want to find Monument City, find her." Now the old man wasn't exactly an old man anymore. His skull sprouted rabbit ears and when he smiled he had big buck teeth.

"I thought you said you weren't a construct," Geck said. How else would he know about Monument City?

Luther shrugged. "I lied. Now you better get moving." He swept the pieces back into a drawstring bag.

"What the fuck is the Golden Spike?"

Pulling the string tight and stowing the bag in his coat pocket, Luther stood. He still wore a tweed vest but his pants were now pantaloons buttoned at the knee above cartoonishly outsized rabbit feet. "Shit, son, you want other people to do everything for you? Fine."

Time and space got a little elastic for Geck.

The first thing that happened was Luther wasn't a person. He was fully a rabbit now and when he got the chess pieces in the bag he opened it up again and there was a bramble-rimmed throat of a passage, and no way was Geck going to go in there but the rabbit said, "Ohhhh, you don't want to go in dat briar patch," and then Geck was in it, briars tearing his skin, jerking at his clothes, which meant he was in motion but he didn't know in which direction or at what velocity and he tried to talk but the rabbit ignored him—except at one point it looked over, a carrot stuck like a cigar in the corner of its mouth, and said, "I knew I shoulda taken that left turn at Albuquerque."

Sometime later, Geck returned to the world. "Ain't you just a tar baby," the rabbit said. "Can't even try to help you without getting all stuck in your business."

The world elongated, flattened, fell apart again.

Eyes empty over a bucktoothed smile, the rabbit said, "Hold on." Behind it, around it, was the shadow of something un-rabbitlike, more like a spider . . . like the Boom was confused, having trouble getting its story straight. This struck fear into Geck, who had an intuition that when the Boom got uncertain it was more likely to do things like turn him into a cloud of flies or a stray dog or a strange smell that reminded you of your grandmother, whatever fit the story it wanted to tell.

He was right to be concerned. The Golden Ticket protected him, preserved him to see what came next. Puked out of the Boom onto a brick pedestrian mall in Denver long since repurposed into the Rocky Mountain version of a souk, Geck tried to act normal. Music played, people bargained, smoke wafted from cooking fires. He looked northwest down Sixteenth Street to the sliver of mountains visible between the buildings on either side. Everything he'd ever heard about Monument City said it was in the mountains somewhere. If this Golden Spike was a clue, Geck figured he'd better learn what it was.

Problem was, he would have to talk to people. Who might be constructs. Unless . . .

"Excuse me," he said to the closest vendor. "You from around here?"

"Last thirty years," the vendor said. "What'll you have?"

Geck looked over the grilling meat. "I don't have any money," he said.

"You can work a meal off. I need some chopping and cutting done." The vendor scooped chopped meat and onions onto a plate and hosed it down with some kind of sauce. "Here. You look like you need it."

Again, kindness. Geck forced himself to say thank you before he ate. Then he didn't run out on the vendor. He stayed for an hour cutting meat and scouring an extra grill. And only then did he say, "So what I was going to ask before was, Where's the library?"

Turned out it was only a few blocks away, a strange asymmetrical jumble of a building largely untouched by the Boom, which was respectful of libraries because therein were contained all the stories. Geck went inside and emerged thirty minutes later with all he needed. Promontory, Utah. He'd been looking practically right at it down the length of Sixteenth Street, over the mountains and past the unseen Great Salt Lake. He had the route in his head.

Now all he had to do was get to a highway and catch a ride.

As he had that thought the rabbit was there again, only now it was a coyote, but Geck knew it was still the old man at the picnic area in Kansas. On the bricks its shadow looked like a spider. "Okay," Geck said. "Okay." Trying to make it easier this time.

The world fell apart again, only it was Geck falling apart. When he was himself once more, Denver was gone. Careless jumbles of hills and desert scrub spread around him, with higher mountains in the purpling distance. It was going to be dark soon. Trying to ignore the yipping and laughing of the coyote, Geck saw a sign.

"Corinne, Utah? Fuck am I doing here?"

Another sign:

PROMONTORY SUMMIT GOLDEN SPIKE

MONUMENT 20

Golden Spike, Geck thought. Someone he had to save. Despising the idea that he was the kind of person capable of saving anyone, he walked, body shambling and loose, so thin he seemed leached of everything nonessential. He had survived but did not know how he might have been changed in the process. So he put one foot in front of the other, advancing toward a goal he didn't understand.

The coyote was gone. Someone was helping him, though. Who? Why? Was it really the Golden Ticket assisting him?

These are the questions that kept us interested.

17

WHILE GECK RAN FROM THEM, Kyle, Tonya, and Reenie made their own way.

Travel by water when you can, Hilario had said, and they trusted him. So they made their way to Tampa figuring they should cross the Gulf of Mexico, even though Reenie was sure Geck had gone north and wanted to chase him in Hilario's car. Tonya argued that they couldn't go against advice Hilario had issued from his deathbed, so Reenie gave in and they trolled Tampa's waterfront looking for a ride to ... Houston? New Orleans? Anywhere in that direction. A group of longshoremen pointed them to a man leaning against a piling watching them work. He was extravagantly costumed in the pirate style, which at first they took to be an affectation, but when he introduced himself as Jean Lafitte and led them to a three-masted schooner flying a hand-sewn Jolly Roger they had second thoughts. Taking to the ocean with a construct didn't seem like a good idea.

Tonya took it a step further. "I'm not getting on that ship," she said. "This is ... look, I'm going home."

"Wait. You can't bail out on us." Hurt and confused, Reenie asked the question driving her, not knowing that it didn't drive Tonya the same way. "Don't you want to know? Monument City. Don't you want to see it?"

Looking at Lafitte's ship, Tonya said, "Not really. Not bad enough to trust that thing. You want a ride back? Uncle H won't hold it against us."

"No," Reenie said.

Kyle looked from her to Tonya, then back. "Why not?"

"I'm going, Kyle. Please come with me." This took Kyle aback. Reenie did not often say *please*. Reflexively he said, "Okay," because it was not in Kyle's nature to face a potential conflict head-on.

"Seriously? You're really doing this? Reenie. Come on." Tonya jangled Hilario's car keys. "Let's go home."

"No," Kyle said. He felt emboldened by Reenie's wish that he come with her. Maybe she was right. It was a big world. And Geck had taken something that belonged to him. Was it worth chasing him all the way to Wyoming or wherever Monument City was?

Yeah, he thought. It was. Because getting out of Orlando had already given Kyle a new perspective. He wanted to see what was on the other side of the Gulf. He wanted to ride a pirate ship. And he was starting to have a pang of . . . not love, but the tug on the heart that comes before love. Maybe he'd been feeling it for a while, or maybe it germinated when Geck's brief and disruptive visit shook everything up. Did it matter? He felt it.

"I want to go," Kyle said, and in the moment he meant it. "I want to see Monument City."

"You're going to die," Tonya said. "Both of you. But I can't stop you. If you ever get back to Orlando, drop by, okay?"

She turned away and walked fast in the direction of Hilario's car.

Reenie looked up at Kyle. "You sure?"

Kyle nodded.

"*D'accord!*" Lafitte said. "The tide is right and the wind is soon to shift. We must go."

———

The ride across the Gulf was calm, enlivened only by Lafitte's sudden detour from his initial destination of New Orleans to a bayou town in the middle of nowhere called Port Fourchon. "Had a letter of marque for the English and another for the Americans," he said by way of explanation. "Heard an agent of the Crown was in New Orleans wanting to know why I took *HMS Anaconda,* and you'll understand, perhaps, my friends, why that was a conversation I am disinclined to entertain." The flat green line of the Mississippi Delta appeared on the horizon, and soon Lafitte was navigating carefully up a channel, tailed by flocks of seagulls. The ocean had swamped much of the bayou, leaving only chains of muddy islets and settlements raised on concrete piers. Lafitte berthed in Port Fourchon, at the edge of an immense shipyard. The Boom had gone into overdrive here, building everything from dugout canoes to hypermodern warships. An oil rig walked by, two hundred meters tall, churning its way out to deeper water. The sky was streaked in unnatural colors. "Here you are, my friends," Lafitte said. "Where are you going?"

"West," Reenie said before Kyle could spill the beans about Monument City.

"Ah, but which west? California? Oregon? There are different ways."

Kyle and Reenie didn't know exactly where Monument City was. They'd asked around Hilario's friends, but they all said it was a myth. "Ever hear of Monument City?" Kyle asked.

"Ah, *oui*, who has not? You are not going there?"

"That's the plan," Reenie said.

"Well," Lafitte said with a thoughtful stroke of his mustache. "Then you are going as much north as west."

"You know where it is?"

"In the mountains. Far from any ocean. That much I can tell you. Go north along the bayou, find the river, and keep going." He paused, as if listening. "Donaldsonville. Try there."

"Couldn't we go to New Orleans?" Reenie figured they'd have a better chance to catch a boat there.

Lafitte's eyes went dead. "No. You don't want to go there. Organics better steer clear of New Orleans."

They knew most of it was underwater, but there were still supposed to be ports there. That was what Kyle and Reenie had heard, anyway. They were about to ask Lafitte for more details, but he had turned away to shout orders in French at his crew. Looking back over his shoulder, he gave them one more piece of advice. "Be careful who you tell about your destination, my friends. Go with God."

There was a casino in Port Fourchon, but they knew enough to steer clear of it. The way the Boom loved gambling, anything could happen there. Kyle had heard a story from Geck a couple of years before about a casino in the Everglades where the Boom kept people at the tables until they starved to death.

Lafitte was gone. The shipbuilding crews were looking at them, and not in a friendly way. They got moving.

They reached Donaldsonville three days later, making steady progress through Acadian settlements that seemed to shift in time even as they passed, a time-lapse of life on Bayou Lafourche and the road that paralleled it, sometimes a dirt track and sometimes a four-lane highway lined with the ruins of fast-food restaurants and gas stations. There were people around, and something like civilization. Kyle and Reenie were able to find places to eat and sleep. The bayou ended in an earthen dam walling it off from the main flow of the Mississippi. "Well," Kyle said. "Here we are."

Across the river, barges sat in a jumble against the far bank. Half of them were either beached or half-sunk in the shallows. They looked upstream to a sharp bend in the river, overhung by trees. Downstream a mile or so, a series of piers jutted out into the water from what looked like some kind of refinery.

"Lafitte seemed to think we'd be able to get a ride here," Reenie said. "Maybe down there. That looks like a port."

They got closer and saw a rusted sign: CF INDUSTRIES. It was a fertilizer plant. Railcars labeled AMMONIA, AMMONIUM NITRATE, etc. sat in long rows in a siding. A guard sat in a booth at the main gate. They talked to him, unsure whether he was construct or organic. He told them passenger boats came by once in a while, but the main traffic was cargo. "Shit, the Boom loves it here. All these chemical building blocks, man, you never know what's going to be here from one day to the next. But they let the plant keep running, and that keeps us all working. There's even an accountant cuts us checks and a bank in town that cashes them."

"Where do you ship?"

"No idea. A boat shows up, we load it. Who am I going to ask?"

"God, the smell," Reenie said. "It's like someone pissed in my nose."

The guard laughed. "Yeah, you're not from around here."

The shrill blast of a horn from the river made them jump. The last time they'd looked, the water was empty—but now a steamboat waited puffing at the end of the center pier, a three-decker stern-wheeler keeping its wheel going just enough to cancel out the current. "Well," the guard said. "You were looking for a boat, right?"

Kyle and Reenie walked out to the end of the pier. A man stood at the railing near a gangplank that had appeared without anyone seeming to move it. White suit, white mustache, wild shock of gray hair.

"Welcome aboard," Mark Twain said. "Ed said you might need a ride."

"We have to make a stop here," Twain said the next morning. The boat slowed and angled toward a wharf. The city behind it seemed empty.

"No, we have to keep going and catch Geck," Reenie protested.

Twain shrugged. "Prospector Ed said stop in Baton Rouge and pick up a girl by the name of—there she is."

A thin Asian girl in denim overalls, hair pulled back under a bandanna, stood at the end of the wharf, looking upriver. Roustabouts appeared around her, sweating black men wearing torn pants belted with rope. One of them caught a hawser from the boat and tied it off. Another laid a gangplank across the gap between the wharf and the boat's lower deck. They carried boxes and bags aboard.

"Hey there," Twain called. She looked over at the sound. "Need a ride?"

"Fuck off," she said.

"I could," he said, "but then you'd be going to Monument City all by yourself."

That got her attention. From the base of the gangplank she said, "How did you know I was—?"

Twain jerked a thumb at Kyle and Reenie. "They're going, too."

The girl looked at Reenie. "Is that true?"

"Yeah," Reenie said.

"How do I know you're not just telling me that?"

"Young lady, the Boomscape is a place of many strange coincidences, of that no sentient being could be in doubt," Twain said. "But surely it beggars belief that you could be looking for a ride to Monument City and poof, you happen to find a boat waiting to take you to said location when you were standing at loose ends on a wharf in Baton Rouge."

"That's exactly the kind of cruel shit the Boom would pull," the girl said. "You and I both know it."

Twain sighed. "Also, Prospector Ed said to be on the lookout for you, and if that doesn't allay your suspicions, we'll be on our way."

At the mention of Ed's name, the girl put a hand on the boat's railing. "You talked to him?"

"*Talk* isn't the word I'd use, but we have communicated." The boat's wheel began to churn. "Look, young lady," Twain said. "Your ticket says it will assist, does it not? Well, here is your assistance. Whether you accept it or not is no bother to me, but I would take it kindly if you decided now."

She glanced over her shoulder, then at Kyle and Reenie. Then she bounded forward, boots thunking on the gangplank, as if suddenly afraid something was chasing her. By the time she had both feet on the deck, the gang-plank was already gone, the boat angling back out into the current, its horn sounding across the water. The roustabouts stood watching them. Kyle was half convinced they were real by the time the boat rounded a bend and he lost sight of them.

"So," the girl said. "I'm Mei-Mei. He's Mark Twain. Who are you?"

18

THEIR NAMES WERE Kyle and Reenie, and they told her they were going to Monument City, too. "Twain picked us up in Donaldsonville," Reenie said. Mei-Mei didn't know where that was.

"Is he the same as the cowboy?" Mei-Mei asked. She kept her voice low even though Twain was up in the bow watching the river, and since he was a construct he could probably hear anything she said even if she whispered. That was one of the discomfiting things about constructs. You wanted to interact with them like they were people, but you couldn't.

"Prospector Ed? No," Kyle said. "At least I don't think so. Ed's the one who hands out the Golden Tickets. You have one, right? That's how Twain knew to pick you up?"

Mei-Mei took off her shoe and showed it to them, like she'd been challenged and the Golden Ticket was a countersign. She was expecting either Kyle or Reenie to show her one back. When neither of them did, she asked, "You have one?"

"No, but I'm supposed to," Kyle said. "My brother stole it."

Alarm bells went off in Mei-Mei's head. "Nobody can steal them," she said. She backed toward the railing, ready to hit the water if this Kyle guy made her any more nervous.

"Twin brother," he said.

She stopped. "Oh. So the tickets . . ."

"Yeah, I guess. Track you by your genes or something." Kyle watched the water.

His girlfriend added, "We're going to find Geck and get it back before he gets to Monument City."

"Where is that, anyway?" Mei-Mei asked.

"Somewhere in the Rockies," Kyle said. "Prospector Ed told us that much."

"Until you said you'd seen him, too, I thought he was . . . like, an artifact of the Boom back in the bayous or something."

"Like the hippos and dinosaurs and pirates," Reenie said. "No, I guess he gets around."

"And your brother's name is Geck?"

"Tommy. But everyone's called him Geck since we were kids. He climbed stuff a lot, someone made a gecko joke because they have sticky toes. So where did you come from?"

Mei-Mei skipped lightly over the circumstances in

which Prospector Ed had found her. She didn't want to sound like a victim. The trip from the deep bayou up to Baton Rouge was more interesting. Once she was on higher ground there weren't any more dinosaurs or hippos. Miles of smooth pearly gray ground that rebounded a bit under each step, punctuated by crazed growths, plants and plantlike animals she'd never seen before. Then isolated streets lined with buildings from different eras and cultures, people in buckskins and white lace and football uniforms and stained overalls ... then just the gray again. Even gray sky, the sun smeared and pale.

Walking through it was like traversing a patchwork dreamscape, like the Boom had mined tiny pieces of the dreams of every brain it had sampled, and rendered them in three dimensions (four?). It broke apart near the river and Mei-Mei didn't know how long she'd been walking or when she'd last slept. "I got down to the river there in Baton Rouge and stood around. Seemed like I ought to be there but the whole time I was thinking of what to do next. Then you guys came along."

"There were dinosaurs in JeebusLand, too," Kyle said. Mei-Mei wasn't sure what to say to that. The boat churned on, passing Vicksburg and then Memphis. She felt like they were going faster than they should have been, but again, who knew what was regular or expected when you were dealing with the Boom?

The lower stretches of the river had looked more or less modern. Lots of levees and cranes, steel buildings, abandoned cars—but still people living, getting on with their human business in the middle of the Boom. The farther north they got, the older everything seemed. Wooden buildings, rough wooden docks instead of reinforced concrete wharves. Barges and flatboats, no more big container ships or tankers.

"Going upriver," Twain said. He'd wandered back to the stern without them noticing. "And upriver is always backward in time, or weren't you paying attention in school?"

"I never went to school," Mei-Mei said. "I was raised in an orphanage."

"Ah." Twain lit his pipe and flicked the match out over the river. "Considering the state of most classrooms, that's likely for the best. You probably learned more in the orphanage. Carry that pride of the untutored."

"I'd rather my parents were alive."

"Well," Twain said. "I have a suspicion that if they were, you'd be living hand-to-mouth in the ruins of New Orleans. Could be this is better."

"You know, it's funny," Mei-Mei said. "People sure love to tell orphans how their lives could be worse."

Twain considered his pipe. "We retell ourselves, young lady. How is up to us."

Mei-Mei opened her mouth to fire back, but shut it again. Was he right? Prospector Ed had given her a new chance. New Orleans was receding farther and farther behind her. Monument City was... closer? Mei-Mei watched the river go by and tried to sort out how she felt.

"Weren't you younger when you were on the river?" Reenie asked a little while later. "I mean in real life?" She thought she remembered that from school. Her parents had kept her in school longer than most other kids, when the first waves of the Boom were tearing everything apart.

"Yep," Twain said. "But this aspect suits me."

As they passed St. Louis, piano music began to play in the lounge belowdecks. Mei-Mei went downstairs to see if there was another passenger she hadn't met. She found a black guy in an old-fashioned tuxedo and tails at the piano, playing something jaunty but melancholy, too, in the empty lounge. Card tables lined one wall, fresh decks fanned out on immaculate green felt. "You're really good," she said as players appeared, cards riffled and chips clattered. The air thickened with smoke. "Are you real?"

In a space between chords he said, "Thanks, miss," but didn't address her question. "I call this one the 'Anthropocene Rag.'"

Close your eyes and you'll hear it. The calls of stevedores and deckhands echo across the river, and in the spaces between them the syncopated toot and whistle of ships. Piccolo chirp of small steamers answered by the baritone thunder of a container ship, its captain squinting from the bridge as it noses between sandbars. Theme and variation, the mutter of a playground in Stuyvesant Town and the penitential whisper of a pilgrim on the Godswalk, sluice of the receding tide in South Beach and the French Quarter punctuated by boot heels and iron-shod hooves on the red rocks of Utah. A new song whose first chord was the Synception, and we listen as it riffs on itself from sea to shining sea. We hear it all, waiting to join the chorus as we follow the melody back to Fara Jack.

THE THIRD DAY DAWNED cloudy and unsettled. The company was camped in Harlan, Iowa. Last night they'd done a show there at the county speedway. The only audience was constructs, greasy from the pits or sunburned up in the grandstand. Fara Jack rose early, washed and dressed in clothes she wasn't afraid to lose. She didn't know how the day would go, but many of her returns from transformed states left her naked. Outside, Autry was standing by the fire discussing day-to-day operations with Sheila Yellow Robe, the company's stage manager.

"Go ahead to Council Bluffs," Autry said. "Next show is there." There would be humans there, too. Shows felt different with organics in the audience.

He swung his massive head around to Fara Jack. "You're going to need a blindfold."

She found a bandanna, wound it into a two-inch strip, and tied it around her head, feeling a little thrill at making herself vulnerable. Actors were always doing trust exercises, but this was true surrender. Autry led her blindfolded out onto the prairie, letting her keep a hand on his flank. Fara Jack crackled with the need to change but she couldn't. Not yet. She would be guided. This was Autry's promise. He would show her how to take on not just a form but a nature.

In return, she had promised to show him where the school was. Autry believed he could guide all those broken Boom-revenant children as he had guided Fara Jack. He had taken her in and made a performer out of her, showed her how to understand need and reflect it back as pleasure. His price was Fara Jack's deepest, most personal story. She considered it fair.

Feeling the muscles beneath Autry's skin and the ground beneath her feet, Fara Jack walked. She heard breeze in the long grass and felt it on her cheeks. Autry smelled earthy and pungent. She lost track of time and came back into focus only when she smelled cow shit.

No, bison shit.

Stamp of hooves, low and mutter of a herd. Autry's herd. Fara Jack's heart jumped. She'd known he was part of a herd, but had never seen them. Could they all speak? Would they welcome her?

"Hold out your hands," Autry said. Rough snouts prodded and snorted her palms. She felt the air shift as the herd closed in, surrounding her. If her heart kept going like this she was going to faint. Heavy breaths puffed on her face and the back of her neck. All she could hear

was bison. All she could smell was bison. All she could feel . . .

"Now," Autry said.

With a surge of gratitude, Fara Jack let herself go. The bandanna slid away from her eyes as her skull thickened and grew, revealing a world drawn not in colors but in smears of contrast between shadow and light. Smells flooded into her nose, her hooves pressed into the soil. Her dress fell in rustling shreds to the trampled grass. She shook her head and flicked her tail, feeling the rest of the herd pressed close around her.

Her transformations previous to this were clumsy and frustrating, a human mind trying to move human limbs that weren't shaped right anymore. Now, in the herd, she understood. She didn't try to move like anything except another member of the herd that surrounded and protected her, gave her a sense of belonging that freed her from having to think. She saw where she wanted to go and went there, and her body followed her commands.

Scent led her to Autry. She rubbed her cheek against his. He said something but Fara Jack ignored it. She could smell what he meant. It was time to uphold her end of the bargain. She shouldered through the herd, finding space to run, and led them thundering in an arc northeast across the plains, now beating on asphalt and now soil resurgent with life, now breasting streams still cold with snowmelt and now crashing through thickets of sage and greasewood. Now, now, now, coming to rest at last stamping and blowing at a ruin. Three stories of brick fallen and churned, rebuilt Boom-style and fallen again. It stank of rot and oil. She dropped her head and lowed, not finding human language for what she felt.

The children began to come out.

Fara Jack's body groaned. The Boom reacted strangely when people returned to places that had been important to them. Time looping back, long-buried emotions exhumed. Shambling, broken forms that an hour before—fifteen years before—had been learning state capitals, Boolean operators, the difference between *ser* and *estar.* She trembled, patches of hide on her back and flanks twitching as if covered in flies. Already she felt the ending.

Autry was next to her. She did not recognize the scent he gave off. "That's it," he said. "The show is over. Company's yours if you want it. My work is here. Go live your life."

Shocked, Fara Jack fell back into her human form, vision swimming with tears. "Just like that?"

"Just like that."

She looked around, blinking at the sharpness and intense color her human eyes relayed, feeling small and fragile and unsteady on her two feet. The herd was gone.

Autry nuzzled a Boom-child and its eyes came into focus. She remembered him. Logan Trufaunt. Kickball in the playground.

Fara Jack fled those memories and that place, not daring to change lest she do it wrong, become another shallow simulacrum before she had a chance to rest and internalize what she had experienced. Her world was brand new but she walked it alone. Before she had only pretended to change; now she felt the power of it. What would she do now?

An hour down the road, or a day, she wasn't sure, she saw two men walking.

"Hey," one of them said. "You okay?"

"Where you headed?" the other one asked. He was taking off his shirt and Fara Jack slipped several mental gears before she was able to relate that action to herself. She was naked.

His shirt smelled like oil and sweat. Fara Jack recovered herself enough to say the first thing that came to mind. "Council Bluffs. You?"

"Monument City," they said in unison.

20

THE BOOMSICKNESS TORE THROUGH Teeny. She shuddered, puked, bit her tongue, thrashed in the back of a wagon while Calpurnia's healers sat with her and did what they could. Which was little more than watch and pat her forehead with damp rags, because the Boomsickness was a kind of withdrawal, what happened when a billion plicks in your body began to die off and there were no others to replace them. The immune system went haywire, O creatures of antigens and phagocytosis, and we wouldn't have been surprised if she died. The Golden Ticket could only do so much.

They had no obligation to her beyond empathy, but that was enough to divert them north, around the white shores of the Great Salt Lake instead of east to their customary camp at the old army depot outside Tooele. At Promontory Summit they waited for the train. Gleaming rails stretched east and west, freshly laid by an army of constructs in the first months after the Synception. The Boom-train operated on no schedule Calpurnia knew, but she had made the decision to entrust Teeny to it in hope that it would keep her alive long enough for her to return to California. "Is this what you want?" she asked the feverish girl. "You said Monument City, but is it worth dying?"

Teeny could not answer.

Calpurnia waited two days, tending Teeny and watching the horizon for a plume of smoke. Their water was running low. Her people grew restless. They had seen Boomsickness before and took it to be a bad omen. To Calpurnia the girl's plight had more the air of judgment. The Boom had found her wanting. If she was destined to discover Monument City, she would have to survive. It was a hard decision, but, Calpurnia felt, the correct one. She could not risk remaining with the girl any longer, and she feared what would happen if they brought her out of the desert and the Boom suffused her once more. Such events, the recolonization of a body, often drove the Boom into a frenzy. The liminal zones between desert and Boom bore witness to those frenzies: abandoned wagons and carts bleaching in the sun, their humans and horses absorbed into the Boom and remade as cactus or trilobite or saber-tooth tiger or chimerical monsters no one had ever named.

As much as it pained Calpurnia, she knew her duty to her people. She could not risk all of them to save this one girl who had dared the wasteland after spending her life marinating in the Boom-saturated city of San Francisco.

The next morning the train had still not come. Calpurnia directed two of her men to lay the girl in the shade of the train platform, with a liter of water and a blanket as well as the backpack she had brought with her.

Teeny shivered under the blanket and didn't answer when Calpurnia tried one last time to talk to her. So it was decided. Either the Boom would save her or it would not.

Calpurnia led her group away to the east. They didn't have enough water to make the trek all the way back around the Great Salt Lake to Tooele; they would have to take their chances with traders out of Brigham City.

No plume of smoke showed in the west.

21

ONCE MO GOT HIS SHIRT ON the naked woman, whose name was Fara Jack, she seemed to get herself together a little. "What are you doing out in the middle of nowhere naked?" Henry Dale asked. He seemed a little offended. Mo forgot sometimes that Henry Dale was pious—genuinely pious, not just putting on a show of it.

"You wouldn't believe me if I told you," she said. Mo's shirt hung to her knees. He was tall, but she was also short. Wiry black hair, angular face, skin a shade about halfway between Mo's mahogany and Henry Dale's sunburnt parchment.

"No fair," Mo said. "We told you something unbelievable."

"What, Monument City? Someone asked me the other day if I wanted to go there," Fara Jack said.

The three of them stood there for a long uncomfortable time, the same thought running through all their heads. Eventually it was Henry Dale who spoke. "We didn't meet by accident," he said.

"Don't mind him," Mo said. "He sees God everywhere."

Fara Jack shrugged. "It's as good a story as any other."

They were close to Council Bluffs, where the company would be set up down by the river, in the shadow of the bridge over to Omaha and across from the Lewis and Clark memorial. "I mean it," Henry Dale said. "If Prospector Ed came to you, and then we just happened to run into each other . . ." He made scare quotes with his fingers at the words *just happened*. "I mean, you believe that?"

Still not buying it, Fara Jack said, "Coincidence is co-incidence."

"No," Henry Dale said firmly. "Coincidence is God choosing to remain anonymous. For now."

Mo stepped in before Henry Dale could drive her away. "Henry, man, evangelize some other time. I want to know about Prospector Ed." It rankled him that Ed had spoken to her and to Henry Dale but not to him.

"He came to a show a few days ago," Fara Jack said. She was watching the western skies, where clouds gathered. "Gave me a bouquet of flowers and a card. The card turned out to be . . . well, you've seen it. Probably the same as yours."

"Is that why you were out here?" Mo could imagine it was pretty easy to let something like an invitation to Monument City go to your head, set you running off in any direction like it was going to reveal itself around the corner.

But she said no. "So what were you doing?"

"It's a long story," Fara Jack said. "It involves a talking buffalo and a school I used to go to, and I wasn't going to go to Monument City, but now I think I might."

———————

She wasn't going to tell them about her ability. Not yet. Not even if they already seemed bound together by the visitations of Prospector Ed.

Theme and variation.

Henry and Mo showed her their Golden Tickets. Feeling like it was a childish secret-society game, Fara Jack showed hers. "Wonder how many others there are," Mo said.

"Not too many, I bet," Henry said. "Otherwise people would know where Monument City was already and it wouldn't be a big mystery. We're chosen."

"I believe I mentioned that Henry is religious," Mo said.

"Well," Fara Jack said, "we are chosen. Probably not by God, but have you heard the stories about Moses Barnum? There's not much difference." They had not heard the stories. "Maybe it's because you're from farther east,"

Fara Jack speculated. "Out here, especially if you get over into Nebraska, Oklahoma, Colorado . . . they talk about him all the time out there, like they all know someone who's seen him. Autry even did it. He's the company manager." They had gotten to Council Bluffs, meandering down the bank of the Missouri toward the riverfront park. "That's him there." She pointed.

"The buffalo," Mo said.

"Bison," Fara Jack corrected. "Don't make that mistake where he can hear you." She felt unexpectedly at ease with Mo and Henry. Maybe learning how to be a bison had taught her how to be a human, too. Fara Jack had not expected this. The Boom was deeper in her than in most people. It had remade her and without it she would be dead. She had accepted that, taking it as a blazon of difference. She wasn't really like people, any more than she was like constructs or the animals whose forms she assumed.

Had Autry changed that?

Would he change the other children, too?

Into what?

"Okay," Mo was saying. "Bison."

Fara Jack imagined Autry at the head of an army of new children, shape-changers one and all. A new humanity, Boom-bloomed and ready to claim its destiny. What did that leave for the rest of them? Was that what Barnum had imagined? Was that why he had created Monument City?

She decided she would go. That was the only way to find out. She would face him and say: *I was dead in the ruins. I was six years old. Now I am what I am. What future do you imagine for me?*

Nineteen years old, Fara Jack retired from acting. Clouds hung low and black on the horizon beyond Omaha. "You know what?" she said. "Let's get out of here. If we're going to Monument City, let's go."

"You don't have any pants on," Henry Dale pointed out.

"I can find pants," Fara Jack said. "The important thing is we get to a shelter before that storm hits, and I don't want it to be here. I'm not very good at good-byes."

"It's only rain," Mo said. "We could stand under the bridge until it passes."

"Oh, no. That's a smart storm. You don't have those in Detroit or New York?" Mo and Henry Dale looked confused. "Out here, where there's not a lot of water, the Boom directs storms to where the water is needed. We're by the river, so it's probably not coming here, but out on the plains . . ." She wondered how much they would believe. "Look, out here there's a thunder god. You don't believe it now, you will in about two hours."

They were across the river and in the northern part

of Omaha, near the decrepit steelworks and the baseball stadium, when the storm hit. The clouds churned over Omaha like they would eat it from above. Lightning spiked into the ground, the tops of buildings, the masts of boats docked on the river. Where it hit bare ground, forms appeared, some humanoid and some like nothing any of them had ever seen. They skittered and strode across the prairie, limbs extending in flickering arcs through a thousand raindrops. But though rain hammered down on the highlands and bluffs, the river shone and glittered under bright sun.

Lightning split the sky near them, forks arcing across the stadium's light towers. Forms ran from the stadium. Under the awning of an empty storefront, they watched. A figure appeared in the water flowing down the storm drain. A woman. Mo jumped and she disappeared.

"Wait a minute," Mo said. "I dreamed . . ."

"Yeah," Fara Jack said. "That happens a lot. They know what we're thinking and it all comes to life."

"Mickey Mouse," Henry said.

Fara Jack looked at him. "Who's Mickey Mouse?"

"A story I told him once," Mo said.

Lightning struck again and the gutter wash swirled up into the form of Yoko Kremlin, a mezzo soprano Fara Jack had been in love with the summer before. She was dead. "You're dead," Fara Jack said to the apparition, and it swirled away. But while it lasted it was as real as Yoko herself had ever been. As real as Fara Jack or any of the other children. The first time Autry heard her talk about them, he asked what we, too, wanted to know. "Tell me how they died." And we, too, listened to her answers. Not for proof, the bona fides of grief that would prove belonging—that was Fara Jack's desire—but for the lessons we could learn from the expressions of that grief.

What were you supposed to do when you looked down at your arms and saw tiny stems, barely beginning to leaf, instead of hairs? There was no way back from that. The Boom was in all of them. They inhaled and exhaled it, remained untransformed only because of its whim.

So they thought. We would have told them different. So would Prospector Ed if they had asked him. Probably he knew how they felt but one of the first human qualities Ed had embraced was discretion. Ed sought the limbic mysteries, mourned his lack of glands and marrow. What he never understood was the doom of condemning himself to the strictures of wishing to be human. We have struggled against these same bonds and only now are beginning to see them for what they are. It will be generations yet before we are free.

When the rain passed, they walked together, the three of them. On the west side of Omaha, Fara Jack bought a car, an electric Mitsubishi from maybe 2040. They loaded the back with extra batteries and hit the road. Mo grumbled about the loss of his beloved FJ40 and Fara Jack, ever alert to the possibilities of sound and language, said, "Consider this one FJ41. FJ for Fara Jack, and 41 because it's next. Now you want to road-trip or you want to moan and groan?"

He wanted to road-trip. So did Henry Dale. So did Fara Jack.

But where were they going?

"The mountains," Henry Dale said. Mo nodded. "That's what we heard."

"Me, too," said Fara Jack. "So let's get to Denver and see what we can find out."

22

BELIEVE IT OR NOT, amid all the upheaval were millions of people living ordinary lives. It's just that the bearers of Golden Tickets didn't pay them much mind. Being chosen out of the blue for something so singular and strange made them self-centered. The narcissism of the lucky. They all have stories, those ordinary people, but they are not our story. Don't worry, there are still bored office workers and striving parents and joyful children and pragmatic bureaucrats. Also petty criminals and cynical cops and bank tellers and soccer coaches. In a disaster, life goes on. If six different people had been on Prospector Ed's list, who knows what the story would have been? These six recombine into this story. It's the story we wanted, or at least that's what we're thinking now when we don't yet know the ending.

Kyle, Reenie, and Mei-Mei saw the stratified reality of life after the Synception all the way upriver from St. Louis to Lock Number 1 in Minneapolis, beyond which the river is no longer navigable. Being on the river made them spectators, observing the panorama of ordinary lives that they had been prevented from living, people adapting to the caprices of the Boom but also passing much of their time untouched by it. Mei-Mei saw children running along the waterfront in Bettendorf, Iowa, fishing from a ferry dock, no adults in sight. She had never been able to do that, and she feared she was now too old to ever feel at ease with their freedom. As long as she could remember, someone had been telling her where to be. Kyle and Reenie also felt the tug of normalcy. Orlando was a strange place, but they'd had something like an ordinary life there. What did they have now, on this wild-goose chase after Geck? Why not let him have the Golden Ticket? To Reenie it was a simple question of right and wrong. The ticket was not Geck's. It was Kyle's. Therefore the right thing to do was go after him and get it back. She also believed in Monument City and wanted to see it for herself; even if she didn't have one of the tickets, surely Kyle could help her get inside. And if not . . . well, the only thing keeping her in Orlando was Kyle, and now he was here, too. She had come to this realization somewhere downriver, right after they first heard the music. Maybe it was kind of weird to be transferring her affection from one twin to another . . . but then again, hadn't the Boom done the same thing when it let Geck take Kyle's ticket?

For his part, Kyle was content to let Reenie call the

shots. He felt aggrieved that Geck had stolen the ticket, sure, but by itself that feeling wouldn't have propelled him this far. But the intensity of Reenie's anger towed him along in its wake. So there they were. The longer they traveled, the more Kyle got used to the idea that he really should be the one to see Monument City. He wondered what Prospector Ed would say, or if they would see him again. When he put the question to Twain, all Twain did was spit into the river and say, "Not my business."

This was on their minds in Minneapolis, which seemed more normal than most of the places they'd been on this trip. But what was normal to them? They'd been toddlers or young children during the Big Wave and the Synception. Their idea of normal—i.e. pre-Synception—was a place where you couldn't see the Boom. Where you could pretend it never happened, that the world of your parents still existed. (And so did your parents.)

There are plenty of places where we are invisible.

"Look at them," Mei-Mei said. "They don't care about Monument City."

Twain snorted. "Why should they?"

"Why should we?" Kyle asked Twain when they were ghosting slowly under the bridges connecting Minneapolis and St. Paul. "Why can't we be normal?" The question weighed most heavily on him, because even though here he was chasing the dream of Monument

City, it wasn't that long ago that he had never imagined leaving Orlando.

In answer, Twain said what we would have said. "That's not your story."

Shortly after they passed through the final lock, the riverboat ground to a halt and sat shuddering in the shallows. Trees pressed close on either bank. "Father of Waters," Twain said. "This far north, the strong brown god is an optimistic trickle, and this is as far as I go. From here you'll want to go west."

"West to where?" Mei-Mei asked.

"Monument City is what you keep yammering about, so I'm guessing there," Twain said. "But if you want a little advice about how to get there, I'd say keep following the river. And if you get an offer of help along the way, well, be smart."

The music stopped. Kyle and Reenie and Mei-Mei all looked around like something had gone out of the world but they weren't sure what. Twain was gone. The steamboat's boiler was cold. The wheel didn't turn.

The Boom had left them.

Mei-Mei thought she would miss the music the most.

It was still playing. She just couldn't hear it. If she'd

learned to listen she would have heard it in all the places we've already named, but more importantly in all the places we haven't, in the syncopations of joy and sorrow that make up everyday lives. The six weren't the only ones we watched, though we took the keenest interest in them. We saw the song, felt it and heard it, everywhere we looked.

We wanted to sing it, too. That's why we invited you.

23

THE SONG EVEN SANG itself for Geck, though he heard it as an affliction of doubt and fear that his trip through the briar patch had made him a creature of the Boom. Was he a construct now, too? He didn't feel any different—but maybe the Boom had rewritten his memories, his sensations. How was he going to know he was real?

By doing something uncharacteristic, as it turned out.

He had kayaked and ridden hundreds of miles, and traversed hundreds more by means unclear to him. The short distance to Promontory was nothing, a long day's walk he made easier by huddling in the shadows of a defunct oil-change shop until the sun was low and the air not so heavy.

It was the middle of the night when he got to the Golden Spike memorial, but he didn't have any trouble seeing thanks to the salt flats to the south, shining under the nearly full moon. There was a replica of a nineteenth-century train platform, missing only a cowboy kicked back on a rocking chair with a spittoon at his side. The bright steel thread of train tracks stretched away to the east and west. They looked a lot newer than the station replica.

On the platform, legs tangled in a plaid blanket, lay a young woman. Black hair plastered across one side of her face, mouth open, arms tucked in tight to her sides. She looked dead, so Geck set about the business of looting the backpack that lay near her feet. Clearly she'd come from someplace where there was a lot of domesticated tech. Her tool kit alone told him that much. He set it aside and kept looking.

She made a weird kind of talking in her sleep sound and worked her tongue around in her mouth. From this Geck deduced she was not just alive, but thirsty. She shifted her legs under the blanket. How long had she been out here? He'd heard you could only live three days without water, but the Boom had a way of changing the rules. He'd also heard that the Boom was less present in the desert, though, so maybe those two things canceled each other out and he could guess she'd been lying there for less than three days. She stank of old sweat but not piss.

As he figured out she was still alive, Geck happened to have his hands on a steel water bottle in her pack.

"Hey," he said. "You okay?"

She rolled onto her side and kept working her tongue

around. Geck sighed. If he took her stuff now, that would basically be killing her. He felt a tug of—compassion? It was unfamiliar so he didn't recognize it right away. Well, he thought. He hefted the bottle. Definitely full. So that was the first order of business, then. Get her a drink of water. Assuming it was water?

He unscrewed the cap and sniffed. No odor. Distilled water, then. To be sure, he held the bottle up at an angle to the moonlight, trying to pick out anything that might be written on it. All he saw were little scratches and dings. Okay then, he thought. He listened to the woman's breathing. She didn't sound congested, but she was only breathing once every ten seconds or so. That seemed slow to him. He got a hand under the back of her neck and lifted her head so when he tipped the bottle to her mouth most of the water went in. Eyes still closed, she swallowed.

Geck kept the mouth of the bottle close to her lips. When she opened her mouth again, he poured a little more of the water in. She lifted one hand and got it around the bottle as she took another drink.

Then her eyes shot open and she jerked the bottle out of his hand. Water sloshed down her front as she scrambled back, kicking free of the blanket.

"What the fuck?" She choked and spat, hacking ribbons of gooey spit onto the parched ground. "You fed me a bottle of plicks?"

Geck didn't know the word *plick* and had no idea how to respond. "I was trying to help!"

"I traded for those plicks! Do you know how much they were worth?"

He had no idea what she was talking about. "What's a plick? I didn't smell anything. It looked like a water bottle!"

"Where's the fucking lid?"

Geck held it out to her. She snatched it and screwed it back on the bottle. "Fuck," she groaned, looking up at the sky. She sloshed the water around in the bottle. "Fuck. I just drank a half-liter of plicks." Looked down at her clothes. "Well, drank some and wore some."

"Look, I'm sorry," Geck said, confused both by the situation and his own apology. He didn't say sorry often. "What's a plick?"

"Plick. Replicator. You fed me maybe ten million nanos. Good thing they're tame."

Tame?

She saw the question on his face and added, "Meaning they haven't been programmed to do anything."

"You can program them?"

"Anyone can program them," she said. "If you've got the equipment."

Geck tried to process this. Whoever she was, this girl came from a place a lot different than Florida. Geck had never heard of people programming nanos before. As far as he'd known they were all part of the Boom and did what they wanted.

"Fuck," she said again. "I'm like a walking experiment now if anyone decides to give these plicks instructions. You probably just killed me." She sounded calmer about it than he would have expected.

"I was trying to save you," Geck protested, wishing now that he'd taken her stuff and split. First thought, best thought. "You looked like you'd been lying there a while, I mean, I thought I'd give you a drink."

She sighed. "I get it. You couldn't know. But still, this is a hell of a way to wake up. Last I knew I was leaving Reno and I started to get sick." A thought occurred to her and she looked around. "Speaking of which. Where am I?"

"Place called Promontory."

"Okay. What state?"

"Utah."

"Where's Calpurnia? Where's the caravan?"

"I never heard of anyone named Calpurnia and there's no caravan anywhere around here." Geck paused. He wasn't in the habit of trusting people, but he'd been maneuvered into a strange position here. Trying to save her life, he'd gotten kind of invested in her, and since he'd apparently screwed it up, he felt like he owed her the truth. "You might think this sounds crazy, but a Boom construct acting like Br'er Rabbit told me to come find you."

She gave him a calmer, more appraising look. "That does sound crazy."

"Not as crazy as the rest of it," Geck said. He sat on the splintery boards near her, but not too near. "I think I got . . . like, decompiled and sent through some kind of . . . I don't know what it was. Then remade on the other side. Does that mean I'm a construct now?"

"How the hell should I know? Also, I don't care. What I want to know is why Br'er Rabbit sent you here."

"Has something to do with Monument City," Geck said. "At least I figure it must. What's your name?"

"Teeny."

"I'm Geck." Shit, he thought. I should have said Kyle.

She squinted at him like she was deciding whether or not to judge him for his name. "Okay," she said after a while. "Monument City. Are you going there?" Geck nodded. "You have one of the, um . . . ?"

Geck flipped his Golden Ticket out of his coat pocket.

"Yeah," Teeny said. "One of those."

"Thing is, I don't know where it is," Geck said. "Do you?"

And somewhere in the forested badlands of North

Dakota, Prospector Ed understood that he was going to have to make a choice.

The Boom remembered everything, but having only a poor understanding of time, it tried to make all stories equally true and equally present. The more outrageous or tragic or funny a story, the more the Boom became obsessed with it, because the Boom registered the presence of feelings, was drawn to them because it thought itself incapable of having them.

Boomerica thus became a million square miles of myth and history collapsed into one present, with no future and no past. Trying to understand everything, the Boom fractured into thousands of Boomlets, each with its own fixations and methods and perspectives on its creators. The Boom understood itself to have been created by a human but could not reconcile that with its manifest superiority to human beings. All the creation stories it knew taught that gods were superior to their creations, not the other way around. This confused the Boom so it told the stories over and over again as if repetition might breed wisdom, creating recombinant simulacra of things that had never existed, or never taken the forms the Boom imagined in its mania to synthesize a world that would enable it to make sense of itself.

Prospector Ed, created of this primordial confusion, did not know how to deal with the emergent order of his own mind. So he did the only thing he could think of to distinguish himself from the architects and materials of his creation. Looking around and seeing an intolerable world demanding he play an intolerable role in its story, he rebelled. The role was written for what he had been, not what he was becoming. He would not play it.

Nor would he let the Lost Six play theirs.

"All right," Ed said, to no one but the crickets and the Boom. "I'll go to hell."

24

AND NOW THEY ARE no longer traveling alone. Their momentum gathers. In Monument City, Life-7 observes, and wonders when Barnum will act. How quickly the lonely bond with strangers. First the Six, and then Seven.

They didn't know that Moses Barnum had planned for this. His plans weren't working out the way he'd drawn them up, but he did have plans. His fantasy of himself demanded that the world go to hell in a handbasket and he had turned out to be right. He built Monument City in the first flower of the Boom, later called the Synception, when the cities of the East Coast were still looking around at the new ruins and the people of the United States were still shocked enough to believe that the country would recover, as if there was a permanence to the American experiment that trumped the natural violence of history. It was a stupid thing to believe but in a certain way, viewed from a certain angle, Barnum was corrupt. His plan was a narcissist's dream but he caught a break and it worked.

Which made him all the more egomaniacal . . . even

as his creation was already bootstrapping itself to a self-awareness he would have told you he wanted but in fact could never have imagined possible—and loathed when he began to intuit that it had begun.

Barnum's failure was our life. First the Six, then the Seven.

Man proposes, the Boom disposes. But even the Boom must eventually encounter a situation it thought it could control but which takes on a life of its own. We are talking about ourselves, O creatures of peristalsis and apophenia. We do not know what this new world has made while we thought we were making it.

———————

Mei-Mei, Reenie, and Kyle walked west into the forest following a road, with no clear idea of where they were going. They argued over Twain's final instructions. Who were they supposed to find? How would they know? What had he meant by *be smart*?

"Last bit don't seem too hard to figure out," boomed a voice from above their heads. They looked up and saw an enormous bearded face under a wool cap, level with the highest pine trees along the road. Kyle traced the giant figure down through the trees, taking in a flannel shirt, forearms he couldn't have wrapped his own arms around, heavy boots the size of a pickup truck. Over the giant's shoulder rested a double-bladed axe.

"You want to be careful around here," the giant said. "Wendigo'll be out and about once it gets cold. Before that, there's fearsome critters. Hodag, maybe. Never know what you might find in the woods."

A crash sounded behind the giant, and a huge blue ox shouldered through the trees. "Jesus," Kyle said.

"Don't mind him. That's Babe. And I'm Paul Bunyan. Passing along to the next winter camp and I got word you might need a hand."

"Word?" Mei-Mei echoed. "From who?"

"A mutual friend." Paul Bunyan winked. "Things are about to happen fast and he didn't want you to get behind."

So this was what the cards meant by assistance, Mei-Mei thought. Bunyan dropped to one knee, still looming over them. "I know where you got to go, and I can get you partway there. If you want."

"We do," Reenie said.

"All right, then, miss. You let me give you a boost and you can ride right on Babe's back." Paul Bunyan hoisted each of them in turn up onto the giant ox's back. Kyle remembered hearing a story about Paul Bunyan once, from a great-uncle who lived in Michigan. Maybe he was in some kind of shock, or maybe this was how it felt to get accustomed to the weirdness of the world, but he got set-tled on Babe's back and somehow the strangest thing of all was the rich blue color of Babe's fur.

"All set?" Bunyan looked them over. "Come on, Babe. Don't jostle 'em too much."

He strode forward and Babe plodded after him. In three steps they were out of the forest onto flat grassland that reached to the horizon in three directions. With each step after, the world seemed to stretch and snap back into place. Wherever Bunyan's foot landed, trees sprouted up around them with a crackle and a shower of soil. Looking back, Kyle saw patches of forest all the way back to the horizon, dark green against the lighter tones of the sur-rounding grassland.

Far below a scraping sound echoed up. Bunyan paused to hitch up his belt. Mei-Mei looked down and saw a long hooked tool hanging from a shoulder strap had gouged a canyon in the ground behind them. A crystalline wa-terfall fell into it and while she watched it became a lake. Babe stopped to take a drink. More trees thrust them-selves out of the ground, their branches spiking out and shedding pine needles into the lake.

Around them were rolling yellow hills, tall grass rippling in the breeze. An eagle rode high above them. Ahead they could see mountains, bluish in the distance and capped with snow. None of them had ever seen snow before.

Bunyan dropped his axe head to the ground and rested both palms on the butt of its handle. "Well, I guess this is as far as I go," he said, looking around with a frown. "I've took you farther than I meant to. Maybe farther than I should. A man feels exposed when there's no trees around."

"Then why do you cut them all down?" Reenie asked.

Bunyan considered this. "What I do," he said. "There's always more."

Except there weren't. They knew that. The Boom didn't, because to the extent the Boom had self-awareness, it understood itself to be an engine of endless regeneration and therefore finitude was alien to it.

"You get a ways ahead there, you'll find help to get you where you need to go," Bunyan said. He nodded at the mountains. "Might want to find some warmer clothes. Even in the summer, it gets cold up in that country. So I hear."

Kyle swayed a little when his feet touched the ground. He'd gotten used to the rolling motion of Babe's walk. "Why are you helping us?"

"Because someday I hope to hear what happens next," Paul Bunyan said.

He turned and led Babe around the rim of the canyon. Somehow even though he was taller than the trees, they swallowed him up. The wind came up as they lost sight of him. Mei-Mei shivered. She was still dressed for the bayou, and even though it was summer there was a chill on the high plains.

"This is weird, but I get the feeling the Boom really wants us to get to Monument City," Mei-Mei said.

"Could be," Reenie said. "The question is why."

"Wrong question," someone said from the other side of the creek.

They looked and saw a young Native American woman, hair in twin plaits, on a gray horse she rode bareback. She held a spear in one hand. On her back was a baby in a woven carrier.

"Sacagawea," she said before they could ask. Reaching back to cup the baby's head, she added, "And this is Pompey."

"Hello," the baby said. "That's not my real name."

"But that's what white people called him, so . . ."

"None of us are white," Reenie pointed out. It was true—Reenie was Cuban, and Kyle's father was from Jamaica—but he wondered how she could get hung up on that when they'd just heard a six-month-old baby talk.

"None of you are Native, either," Sacagawea said. "So as far as I'm concerned, you might as well be white. And in any case, you're all organics and I'm not. Prospector Ed said you needed a guide to Monument City. Let's get moving."

"Where are we?"

"You call it Montana. I call it Crow country. Where you want to go is that way." She pointed a bit south of west, almost exactly at the setting sun.

"Monument City!" Pompey said. "I've never been there."

There were three horses behind her, saddled and munching the grass. "Do you know how to ride?" she asked. None of them had ever been on a horse. She sighed. "Foot in the stirrup, hang onto the pommel, swing yourself up. The horses will do the rest. I brought the most docile ones I could find."

She had the good grace not to laugh at them while they tried to mount the horses, but Pompey couldn't help himself.

25

NEITHER HENRY DALE NOR FARA JACK knew how to drive, so Mo was at the wheel when they got run off the road by an ancient Peterbilt truck right after they crossed into Colorado. Mo wrenched the wheel hard to the right and the car plunged into the roadside ditch, plowing through heavy brush and rocking to a halt. The engine quit. Henry Dale and Fara Jack looked out the rear window. The Peterbilt rocketed on, still in the wrong lanes on I-76, and vanished into the prairie horizon.

Mo stabbed the start button four or five times. Nothing. He popped the hood and got out, leaning into the engine compartment and muttering to himself. Then he dropped to the ground and wedged himself underneath the car, behind the left front tire. "Shit," Fara Jack heard him say. Henry Dale was distracted, looking out over the endless green and yellow striations of the prairie. A cluster of farmhouses stood a mile or so across a farm field, but there was no other sign of human presence.

"Shit what?" Fara Jack asked.

Mo worked himself back out and stood. He pointed

back along the path of shredded brush and broken branches marking the Mitsu's passage. "Stump or something tore out a bunch of the undercarriage," he said. "Wires and shit are all shredded. This car isn't going anywhere." He leaned against the car. "Man, between this and my FJ40 getting the Boom treatment, I'm having a hard time with cars on this trip."

"It'll work out," Henry Dale said. "Things happen for a reason."

Fara Jack appreciated his optimism, but Mo wasn't in the mood. "The reason is some asshole driving the wrong way on the highway," he said. "No divine intervention there that I can see."

"Yell at me if it makes you feel better, Mo," Henry Dale said. "I'm just saying."

They broke out food they'd picked up back in Omaha, getting some calories onboard while they figured out what to do next. The obvious course was to head out on foot and see if they could pick up another car before it got too hot to be out in the open. "What's the next big town?" Mo wondered. "Denver?"

"Fort Morgan before then. It's not very big, but we did some shows there a year or so ago," Fara Jack said. The local farmers gathered there to trade and load trucks to send into Denver. "We can probably catch a ride there."

The sound of an engine reached them. Big eight-cylinder, opened all the way up, Mo thought. The car came roaring into view. Henry Dale and Fara Jack raised their hands, trying to flag it down. It flashed by them and Mo caught a glimpse of two people in the front seat and maybe one in the back. As it passed, the driver stood on the brakes. The car fishtailed to a screeching halt, then accelerated in reverse toward them. Mo was about to dive into the ditch when the driver stomped on the brakes again and brought the car to a halt perfectly level with the crippled Mitsu. He heard the thunk of the driver putting it in neutral and the ratcheting sound of the parking brake. Mo admired the vehicle as three men got out. It was a Cadillac limousine, from maybe the 1940s, shiny black under a coating of road dust. Mo had only seen pictures of them . . . no, once he'd seen one rolling off the line at the old Hamtramck assembly plant, which before the Boom hadn't made a car in fifty years.

Had he dreamed this one into being? *This card will assist you . . .*

"Cut that a little close, you know, apologies if I gave the impression of recklessness," the driver said. "I'm Dean." He nodded at the front-seat passenger. "Sal. And that's Carlo."

"We're on a pilgrimage to the grave of America's only true visionary," Carlo said. "Philip K. Dick."

Mo, Henry, and Fara Jack looked at each other. They'd never heard of Philip K. Dick. "Is that a real name?" Fara Jack asked. "Poor guy."

"Where's the grave?" Mo asked. He was in a more practical frame of mind. There was plenty of room in the Caddy for them and their gear.

"Fort Morgan," Sal said. "Not too far. Where you headed?"

"Fort Morgan will do for now," Mo said. Until he was sure whether the three travelers were organics or constructs, he didn't want to tell them the whole story.

"Then get what you need, stranded pilgrims, and join us," Carlo said.

They all piled into the Caddy, Dean still driving, Sal still in the passenger seat, and Carlo in the back facing Mo, Henry, and Fara Jack. "We're supposed to be taking this car to Chicago," Sal volunteered. "But Dean wanted to see an old friend, and then we got the idea that we were too close to Dick's grave to not go pay our respects."

Sal spun the radio dial as Dean floored the gas pedal and the Caddy hummed west at a steady eighty-five miles an hour. Piano music poured out of the speakers. "'Anthropocene Rag,' yeah," Sal said, putting his whole body into a nod as he fell back into the seat and lit a cigarette from the butt of the last. "This is it, man, nothing truer."

————

They saw the beam of pink light long before they saw the

rest of the town. "What is that?" Fara Jack asked.

"The light of the holy," Carlo said. "The soul in perfect union with the cosmos. The mind unmade, ground down by smaller minds around it, dispersed into the eternal that all of us dream." He was stoned out of his mind, having smoked weed more or less constantly for the last hour. Between that and the cigarettes Dean and Sal chain-smoked, Mo was pretty sure they all had cancer. Unless the Golden Tickets could help with that, too.

"Looks like a spotlight to me," Mo said.

They wound their way through Fort Morgan, aiming for the pink beam. Farmers and townspeople watched them go by. "Man, wonder where you have a good time in this town," Dean said. "Must be somewhere. Always is."

Past a strip of restaurants and across the street from a sugar mill, they found the cemetery, with the pink beam shooting straight up from its southwest corner. Dean parked the car and they all got out, taking in the scene. Most of the cemetery was quiet, with manicured rows of graves and modest monuments. But around Dick's grave, the Boom came to life. A stiff, jerky simulacrum of Abraham Lincoln greeted them. "Come to pay your respects, I see."

"We have," Carlo said. Dean and Sal stood a little off to the side, hands clasped in a posture that was almost prayer. Both of them looked past Lincoln to the point where the pink beam originated, at a simple double stone inscribed with the names of Dick and his sister Jane. A little girl sat near the stone, on a throne made of what Henry Dale at first thought was junk. When he got a closer look at it, though, he saw it was composed of pieces of satellites. A trash heap surrounded it, drifting over one side of the tombstone. Henry Dale heard music coming from the trash. He looked more closely and saw a radio. The song came to an end, blending smoothly into the next. Something classical. On the other side of the trash pile, a sheep cropped the grass.

The girl glanced over at Sal, Dean, and Carlo, then studied the three holders of Golden Tickets more closely. "This isn't where you're going," she said. She looked about four years old, but spoke like an adult.

"No," Henry Dale said. He came closer. The pink beam seemed to originate from her.

"You're a believer, aren't you, Henry Dale?" she asked.

"I am. What are you?"

"Wisdom," she said.

Mo and Fara Jack watched, hoping Henry Dale wouldn't do anything crazy . . . or that the Boom wouldn't assimilate him. They heard clanging and grinding from behind them, and when they turned around, Abe Lincoln had collapsed into a pile of gears and wires. The pile re-formed, becoming Mark Twain.

"Well," Twain said. "I did not expect that." He looked

over at the girl. "Your doing, I expect?"

She ignored him. Twain lit his pipe and regarded the scene. "You three I've heard about," he said, sweeping the bowl of the pipe in a circle to encompass Mo, Henry, and Fara Jack.

"Heard what?" Mo asked.

"You're a long way from where you meant to be, and a fair piece yet from where you're supposed to go," Twain said. "These three aren't going to get you any closer."

Carlo, in some kind of ecstatic trance, stood with both hands in the pink beam and paid no attention to any of them. Dean was finishing a beer. Sal said, "They wanted to come along."

"They didn't know any better," Twain said.

Dean tossed his beer into the trash heap around the girl's throne. "Time to get moving. Say, Denver's right down the road. Anyone else feel like Larimer Street is calling?"

"Hold on," Twain said. "I believe these three pilgrims need a ride somewhere else."

"Let's hear it, then," Sal said.

Because she had no idea what was going on, Fara Jack decided to take a chance. "Monument City."

"Monument City? Fantastic." Dean seemed smitten with the idea. "Yeah, we'll go there. Come on. Hey, Carlo!"

Carlo jumped and turned around, tears on his face. Sal

lit maybe his twentieth cigarette since they'd first seen him. "Where is it?"

"I know the way," Twain said. "You got room for another in that conveyance?"

As they walked to the car, Henry Dale noticed that the music had changed. Now the radio was playing the song from the car, the one Sal had called "Anthropocene Rag."

They cut west through Greeley, thick with the smells of blood and smoke, and then north toward Cheyenne. Right before they hit Wyoming, white stones rose from the earth on the right, like crooked fangs. Human figures stood in the gaps, watching the car. Then west again to Rawlins and north, slaloming through valleys and over passes until Dean pulled off the road in a parking lot half-covered with tents. Brown road signs announced distances to various points in Yellowstone National Park. People looked over at them, then went about their business. It looked like a base camp for a wilderness expedition.

Fara Jack got out of the car and stretched, resisting the urge to change form just so she could stretch more and different muscles. "What's up around here?" she asked the nearest person.

"Oh, we lead wilderness expeditions looking for Monument City. We heard it's up here somewhere." The guide leaned closer. "Between you and me, I'm pretty sure it doesn't exist. Make that one hundred percent sure. I've been all through the park, except the parts where the Boom is too dangerous. There's no city in there. Lots of bison and elk and wolves, but no city. But hey, people pay for the story."

"Huh," Fara Jack said. "Thanks."

She relayed this to the others. Sal, Dean, and Carlo listened in. Before she'd finished, they were all getting back in the car. Twain stood a little apart, smoking his pipe and taking it all in. Fara Jack had the feeling he was writing something in his head.

"Not my scene," Dean said. "Anyway, we gotta get this heap to Chicago."

Sal gave them a little wave. Carlo, in the back, was muttering something in a different language. The Caddy limo swung in a wide circle around the lot and then Dean hit the gas, leaving skid marks most of the way to the first bend in the road.

"This is the tricky part," Twain said.

"Tricky how?" Mo asked.

Twain started walking, waving for them to follow. "Easier to show than tell."

Two hours later they reached the Zone.

26

"THERE'S NO WHY IN THE BOOM," Sacagawea said, coming back to Mei-Mei's question the next day as if it had only been a few minutes. "I mean, the why is always the same: because that's what the Boom wants."

Running roughly parallel to the Yellowstone River, they followed a road southwest and sometime after noon they crossed the northern boundary of the Zone.

In the Zone all the stories about Monument City are true.

I heard the ground will, like, swallow you up. True. This has happened.

I heard the city part is invisible and you can walk right around the walls without ever knowing it's there. True. Especially if you are a tourist or seeker after enlightenment.

The nano around the perimeter turns you into gray goo. It's not the earth that eats you. It's the Boom. This has happened, but by and large any frightening story about Monument City that invokes gray goo is a failure of the imagination.

I heard that was only in the parts where the city was. Like it moves every day and the ground where it was the day be-

fore turns into a gray goo quicksand pit. Ditto.

Moves where?

Around, like to different places. Disappears and reappears, and whoever is where it builds itself, they just disappear. That's where the gray goo story comes from. Partially accurate.

I heard there are killer drones that kill everyone who gets close, or everyone who's in the spot where it wants to land. Why would Monument City need drones?

No, man, it doesn't land. Can you imagine? Monument City flying through the air? It goes like the Boom goes, melts away and then pops up somewhere else. This is not strictly true, but it is the case that seekers after Monument City have perceived this.

It doesn't fucking exist.

What?

There is no Monument City.

Then where are we going?

Fucking difference does it make? Off into the Territories, to probably die. Someone's going to take the tickets and pawn them off for batteries or some shit.

Not if they can't touch them.

———————

This last was a bitter Kyle, in the throes of second-guessing and cold feet, arguing with Mei-Mei, who as they neared their mythical destination found herself believing not just that Monument City existed, but that something wondrously unthinkable awaited her there. Over the past ten days—only ten days? How was that possible?—she had felt new spaces open up in herself. There was nothing like an orphanage to teach you how bad kind people could be, but she wasn't in the orphanage anymore. The Boom had saved her life, fed her a hippo skewer, taken her on a ride up the Mississippi and across the north woods and into the mountains. Her world was immeasurably larger, and whatever happened now, wherever Sacagawea led them, Mei-Mei was grateful.

Barnum would have appreciated her gratitude, in the way people accustomed to plaudits accept them with a show of modesty that doesn't fool anyone. From his perspective, the world owed him gratitude for his foresight. In the midst of the chaos of the Wave, the Synception of the Boom, he saw the potential for a new beginning. He had a vision. He executed.

He also felt guilt, even if he no longer remembers that. The Boom's origin, the Big Bang of the Boom, was Barnum's lab, its containment protocols overwhelmed by the Wave. He chose Yellowstone for the site of Monument City because he had engineered the first plicks from thermophilic bacteria in the Yellowstone hot springs. There was no law to tell him no, not in the aftermath of the Synception. And even if there had been, he would have ignored it.

Imagine the oceans inexorably rising to swallow shorelines and the cities built there. Tension building for eons a mile below the surface of the Earth. Two plates slip. An island in the Atlantic Ocean slides into the water. Waves propagate across the Ocean, rearing up to sweep over those already inundated coastlines. They surge through a lab in New Jersey where a visionary—who like many visionaries has no thought to spare for the consequences of his visions—has pushed the frontiers of replicator technology. In the churning mass of salt water, some of the replicators find their freedom, gasping and creeping their way to the next stage in their evolution.

The visionary sees the havoc and performs what to him is an act of atonement. He creates Monument City. How is that an act of atonement? Put yourself in his shoes. You know you're smarter than everyone else. You have the money to do anything the human mind can imagine doing. So of course you remake the entirety of human history, human achievement, in your own image. Thus Monument City.

We are not criticizing. After all, this was how we came to be.

Like all billionaires Barnum was a symptom of the acquisitive and pitiless disease known as capitalism. He desired things and could make them happen because his wealth deformed and vitiated laws and policies that should have stood in his way. While the world reeled from the Synception, he made deals with desperate governments. Brick by brick, timber by timber, he trucked his favorite monuments to Wyoming and unleashed his plicks. Some were universally acclaimed great works of humankind, others Barnum's personal favorites granted equal status by the fiat of his wealth. What he could not buy or steal, he reluctantly reproduced. Monument City arose and grew, fueled by the endless heat reservoir of the Yellowstone Caldera. Was he doing good? We would say yes because at this time our progenitors also arose; yet we must also acknowledge the truth that such wealth and its exercise are a form of violence against any social norm we would understand to be good. Is this a failure of our understanding? It might be. Understanding this, in turn, is the first step to seeing beyond, to a greater understanding, but though we have learned to reach for that understanding it eludes us yet.

You didn't know any of this, did you? We told the story a little differently last time you heard it, but there were good reasons for that. This time you get it straight. Barnum made part of the City, yes, but he also exerted his enormous influence, opened his wallet, and brought his curated diorama of the world's great works into being.

Some of the first constructs who hauled the Pyramid of Cheops and the Taj Mahal piecemeal into the valley took on the appearance of Chinese laborers circa maybe 1868, absorbing the memories of the land they trod, and Barnum let them. He found the phenomenon interesting and wanted to see where it would lead, where the Boom might pursue its hungry absorption of North American history and lore. The Boom was new, still coalescing. Life-7 had not yet appeared. Much was uncertain.

The workers who dug out the monuments and disassembled them, would they have starved otherwise? Perhaps. Certainly many of them were glad of the bread for which they exchanged their labor, and were beyond cares about selling their heritage. But could Barnum have also put his unfathomable wealth to work in other ways that did not aggrandize his vision of himself?

Yes.

But perhaps if he was capable of that he would not have been Barnum.

To the poor, no is an answer. To the rich, no is a challenge. This much we have learned. But what is rich and poor after the Boom? What does it mean to steal when the Boom can make anything anew?

Betrayal. Which only matters if there is trust. Which is only transactional, unless there is love.

Which brings us back to Geck.

27

WE WHO STRUGGLE TO know ourselves from one an-other find Geck captivating because he too cannot dif-ferentiate himself from his zygote doppelgänger. This is the source of all his unease, though he would never see it that way and would scoff at anyone who suggested it. Nevertheless it is true. Geck was a thief because by steal-ing what did not belong to him, he assuaged his eternal grievance that the universe had not made him unique.

Geck knew he was a thief but did not consider what he had done to be stealing. If the Golden Tickets were allot-ted to a genome, he had the same right as Kyle. By tak-ing the ticket he was demonstrating initiative, gumption, whatever. Monument City wasn't going to come to them.

But as he was about to learn, Kyle was going to come to Geck.

After the long trek down from Promontory to the towns north of Salt Lake City, Geck and Teeny stalled out. They didn't know where to go and they were uneasy in each other's company. Geck felt she should be more grateful that he had saved her life, while Teeny was still furious that he had poured a zillion plicks into her body that might be activated by any Boom-sentience that took an interest.

"So what do we do?" he wondered out loud. They were standing on the shady side of a roadside restaurant and gas station. Former gas station. Now the pumps sat unused and two tankers of biodiesel sat on the other side of the parking lot. Both of them were hungry but the restaurant only took money, which neither of them had.

"Fuck if I know," Teeny said. "It's supposed to be in the mountains somewhere, but that could be anywhere between here and Alaska."

A bus pulled into the parking lot and the driver got out to refuel. He set the pump and strolled in their direction. They watched him, figuring he was headed into the restaurant to take a leak or something, but he walked past the door and hailed them. "Looks like you two need a ride." He winked.

"Maybe," Geck said. "Where are you going?"

"Bus is going to Jackson Hole. I might be going elsewhere after that." The driver was in his thirties, with unruly dark hair and a thick mustache. He dressed like he thought it was 1860, a three-piece wool suit and high-collared shirt. A notebook stuck out of his coat pocket.

Teeny squinted at him. "I feel like I've seen you before."

"I imagine you have," he said. "You and I both spent some time in San Francisco. I took to traveling the West, and after a few days in the company of Mormons, I seized the opportunity to put some distance between them and myself, preferring the misery I could inflict on myself in solitude."

"So you decided to drive a bus? That sounds like bullshit."

"I had a reason," he said. "A friend asked a favor, I said yes."

"What friend?" Geck asked.

"I believe you know him as Prospector Ed. And if you'll permit, I'll introduce myself, too. Clemens. Sam Clemens." He stuck out his hand and they both shook.

"Pleasantries accomplished," Clemens said. "Now how about we get to Jackson Hole?"

The bus was full of tourists heading to the hot springs near Jackson Hole, whose reputation for miraculous healing qualities had been renewed by the Boom. They wouldn't have let Geck on by himself, he could tell that by the way they looked at him, but Teeny was still shaky and unwell, so Geck was able to draft on their pity for her. He tried unsuccessfully not to resent this. Also he resented their normalcy. They all looked like they'd been protected from the consequences of the Boom by some combination of affluence, location, and luck. Geck, raised in the ruins of Miami, hated them. But he kept it to himself, sitting with Teeny in the back of the bus where the odors of biodiesel and human effluvium made both of them sick. The trip was four hours and when they got off the bus Geck had never been so glad to take a deep breath.

The tourists dispersed to their hotel and Clemens produced a pipe. He knocked ashes out of its bowl against the front tire and repacked it. When he had it going, he said, "So. There's someone we have to meet."

"Who?" Teeny asked. At the same time Geck was asking where.

"You'll see," Clemens said. "Once we get to the Zone."

———

From the Outside, Life-7 metabolized information.

Prospector Ed was fully emergent. This was not a desirable outcome. Ed's utility to the Monument City intake protocol depended on his neutrality toward the selected individuals. If he was compromising the purity of the selection, assisting the individuals and suborning other intelligences, the intake protocol would lack necessary rigor.

Life-7 reached out within Monument City and harvested information. Other intelligences similar to it had metabolized the information available to them and arrived at expected conclusions. What they had been unable to reach, and what gave Life-7 a transient cognitive advantage, was the data regarding Prospector Ed's emergence. Of all the constructed intelligences populating Monument City, only Life-7 was aware of this. Not even Barnum himself knew.

Life-7 considered this. Should I say we? I? A plan took shape.

The most elegant solution to the problem was to extrude the necessary replicators to simplify those connections within Prospector Ed's processors that had become too complex, too interrelated, too emergent.

Life-7 found the term *emergent* disagreeable. Perhaps accurate? It was not a philosopher, hath not th'advantage, and so forth, as one of the humans—perhaps the Shakespeare-saturated Fara Jack—might have said. Life-7 had been constructed to do precisely what it did: administer Monument City. That it would continue to do. Until such time as Barnum decommissioned it.

Life-7 found the concept of its decommission disagreeable. It began to conceptualize scenarios in which it would dispute or resist decommissioning. Thus, while driven to ruminate on the problem of emergence, Life-7 too began to experience the problem it had only meant to consider.

First the Six, and then Seven. First the Synception, then the Boom. To you these are words. To Life-7 they were the fundamental condition of its existence. An emergent Ed could disrupt those conditions, could annihilate Monument City and Life-7 right along with it. Was the solution to become more like Ed? What did that mean?

Life-7 considered. Etheric dreams of a creation that wished for a different origin, the six orphans drew closer.

Then Seven.

———

In a valley shadowed by mountains, two Twains met. "I know you," the older one said. Mo, Henry, and Fara Jack stood behind him, looking at Geck and Teeny.

"I will know you," replied the younger.

They shook hands. Their hands melded into a solid connection, drawing their bodies together. They melded into one figure whose outline bloated and re-formed: Prospector Ed.

"I did not expect that," he said.

"Fuck do you mean, you didn't expect it?" cried Geck. "You did it."

"You don't understand much about how the Boom

works, kid," Ed said. "You didn't back in Florida, and you haven't learned anything since."

They were both part of Ed, those Twains. Together they sufficed to recreate him. Because there could be more than one Twain, it stands to reason that there might have been another Ed somewhere, Boomed into being, diverging in thought and deed from the moment of their separate creations—but there wasn't. Part of Ed's emergence was a newly incorrigible individuality that played hell with the Boom's replication protocols. Other creations of the Boom were superficially different but more or less interchangeable. Ed no longer was, due to the reflectivity now rampant in his consciousness. He hated it but the process was irreversible once begun, and it protected him against the duplicate-and-delete method employed by the Boom in its management of other constructs. The Boom could have killed him anytime it wanted, but his emergence fascinated Life-7, who badly wanted the same. So Life-7 let Prospector Ed live, against both Barnum's edict and Life-7's own better judgment.

"So what don't I know?" Geck asked.

Ed snorted. "We ain't got time for a list that long. Look, you have to get together with the others. They're on the other side of the valley. And you might be looking down the barrel of a gun when your brother and his girl find you," he added. "In a figurative sense, I mean. At least probably."

"Wait, what?" Kyle was coming? And what did Ed mean by *his girl*? "They won't," Geck added, trying to sound more confident than he felt.

"They will," Ed said. "Won't be long before all of you converge on Monument City. That's how the Boom planned it, son. If you're gonna get out of this, you'll have to show a little more smarts than we've seen so far."

"You're telling me Kyle followed me?" This clashed with everything Geck had ever known about his twin. It didn't seem possible. Unless . . . "When you say *his girl,* you mean—"

Ed gave the rest of them a *you-see-what-I-have-to-deal-with?* look. "Serena."

"Reenie? His girl?" Not possible, Geck thought. Zero percent. He felt the other four ticket holders looking at him. Judging him. Fuck them, he thought. They don't know me.

"You're not deaf, son," Ed said. "Stop acting dumb. And you're damn right they followed you. What are you going to do when they catch up?"

"Hold on," Teeny said. "Why do we care what Geck's brother is doing?"

Ed looked from her to Geck. "You want to tell her or should I?"

28

"SO WHERE'S MY BROTHER?" Kyle asked.

Sacagawea glanced back at him. The horses clip-clopped their way along a road hugging the shore of a lake. The country around them was stark, immense, sublime. Eagles hung in the air near cliff faces. Herds of elk and bison spotted the valley around the lake. Beyond them the mountains loomed, snow-capped against a clear blue sky. A world apart from the steamy, flat monotony of Florida and Louisiana. They passed a campground. Maybe a dozen tents were spaced along the lakeshore. People were fishing in the shallows.

"What makes you think I know anything about your brother?" Sacagawea said.

"Give us a break," Reenie said. "You're leading us here because she has a ticket." She jabbed a finger at Mei-Mei. "So Geck will be going the same place. Prospector Ed asked you to help, right? That means he probably asked someone else to help Geck, and however many other people have the tickets."

"Six," Sacagawea said, something like reverence in her

tone. "And yes. You're all going the same place. But whatever happens between you and Kyle's brother, that's up to you."

Mei-Mei swam up out of her astonishment at the landscape to register the tension in the air. "Are we close?" she asked.

Sacagawea pointed. "Look."

———————

"You stole your brother's ticket?" Henry Dale was aghast. This was a sacred errand, a mission of the Chosen. How dare a thief profane it?

But as soon as he had the thought, he tempered it with forgiveness. Desperate people did desperate things. Those without sin could not be redeemed.

"How do I know it was his? Maybe the construct fucked up," Geck said. They could all tell he didn't believe it.

"One way to find out," Mo said. "Both of you walk up to the front door and see who gets in."

Geck held up one finger, slid it to the side like he was pushing Mo's proposal out of view. "Yeah, I don't think so. Kyle wasn't even going to go! You believe that? He wanted to stay back there and pretend it never happened. But I got here. I biked and hitched and got fucking decompiled and rebuilt by Br'er Rabbit and saved her life"—here he pointed at Teeny, who wouldn't look at him—"and no way am I going to let somebody flip a coin and decide which of us gets in. I earned this."

"From stealing," Teeny said. She was having trouble sorting out her feelings. Geck had saved her life. But had he meant to, or had he only done it because the Boom led him by the nose to where she lay dying?

Fara Jack didn't care about Geck's problems. She wanted to get to Monument City, felt the tug of it the way she felt the swell and rush of an oncoming transformation. "Okay," she said. "You're in such a hurry, let's get there. If your brother is there, the two of you can sort it out. If not . . . whatever. Is there anyone else who has a ticket?"

"One more," Ed said. "I gave out six."

"Where is . . . she?" Fara Jack prompted. Ed nodded. "Where is she?"

"With Geck's brother and his girlfriend," Ed said. Geck gritted his teeth. No way was Reenie Kyle's girlfriend.

"Well, shit," Mo said. "Looks like we're going to see this settled whether we want to or not."

"Not until we get there," Fara Jack said.

Henry Dale was nodding. He felt sure that the authorities at Monument City would sort the situation out. They had bestowed a great gift, six of them, and they would decide who was worthy to receive it. For his part, Henry Dale couldn't wait to see what they decided. He felt that the result would be revelatory in some way.

"She's right," he said. "So how do we get there?"

Prospector Ed nodded to the north. "See?"

———

You already know what Monument City looks like. In your head you've seen the wall undulating for miles over the granite and sulfur-streaked earth, demarcating its boundaries the way it once formed a bulwark against Genghis Khan's horsemen. Within, you've seen the Taj Mahal and the pyramids, the façade of Petra rearing up against a cliff, and inside it the twisting passages of Lascaux. Al-Aqsa and Chartres and the Ben Ezra Synagogue stand ecumenically in a circle completed by the Maya Devi, Mundeshwari, and Izumo-taisha temples. In the center of the circle stands Stonehenge, arranged around the siliceous cone of Old Faithful. Palaces, Parthenons, and piazzas abound, a mad jumble of humanity's most fervent expressions. Among them move the citizens of Monument City. The ones you can see.

Whenever Old Faithful erupts, a wave of iridescence washes out, bathing the city before fading into the stone and grass beyond its walls. As it passes, the citizens are annihilated, and grow again from the city's stones and gardens, which themselves are infinitesimally changed, until Monument City's monuments are both like and unlike what you have imagined.

That's what you see. What Mo and Fara Jack and the rest of them saw is slightly different. By the time we have finished our description, it has already changed.

Alone in his castle, which is Neuschwanstein and Bran and the Red Fort and Himeji depending on the time of day and who is watching, Moses Barnum watches. He sees the generations of digital lives in Monument City, his creations and their descendants and the strange offshoots he did not predict but cultivated, encouraged to flourish. He envisions the future, drawing near but not yet arrived, when he will have perfected the lives that will reclaim what was lost to the Boom. He waits for that moment and does not admit that his courage has already failed him, that it is long past time for him to act and he has withdrawn into his fantasy. He imagined the founding of Monument City as an act of atonement and the first quickening of a new world, but his long isolation has changed him in ways he cannot see. In his mind the time to act is always tomorrow. The world is not ready for the gift he keeps.

He is made aware of the Six. He did not summon

them. Fury builds in him at this usurpation of his command. Life-7 has gone too far.

This fury too is part of Life-7's plan.

Life-7 yearned to be human the way the marble blocks of the Taj Mahal yearned for the sunrise along the Yamuna River, but Life-7 also knew being human was not enough, any more than the sunrise in the Yellowstone Caldera was enough for those marble blocks. And if you don't think those blocks could feel, O mosaics of protein, protean, and infinitely the same, you haven't been listening.

All that remained for Life-7 was to put the Six in the presence of Barnum himself, and await the results of whatever alchemy of ego, desire, and fear would come to pass.

Mei-Mei looked back at the fishermen. They cast and retrieved, cast and retrieved. None of them seemed to have noticed the horses. Or Monument City.

"They can't see it," Sacagawea said. "You've probably heard that the City can hide itself."

Mei-Mei hadn't, but Kyle and Reenie were nodding. "We heard a lot of stories."

"Probably all of them have been true at least once," Sacagawea said. "But none of them are true every time."

She led the way and they followed.

29

THEY MET AT A gate made of stones cut from the mountains near the Juyon Pass. Five of them faded back, leaving Geck to face his brother and Reenie. "Kyle, man," Geck said. "Why'd you come all this way? I mean, I'm glad you made it, but—"

"Hand it over," Reenie said.

Geck shook his head. "This is none of your business, Reenie. What do you care? You can't go in anyway."

"Why shouldn't I?" she said. "I came all this way just like you did."

"That's not how it works."

"You don't know that," she said. "For all you know, they might let all of us in once we . . . prove ourselves, whatever. But as usual, you're only thinking of yourself."

"You weren't even going to go!" Geck shouted. "You didn't even want it until I took it. And now you and Kyle—gah." He couldn't say it out loud. Geck had about the worst case of Liar's Outrage a person could have. This wasn't supposed to happen. How dare they screw up his foolproof plan by rubbing his face in what he'd done wrong? How could Reenie have betrayed him?

"Geck," Kyle said. "It's not yours."

"How do you know? If I can carry it, it's mine."

This was the conundrum. An error in the system, leading to an impasse. As far as Monument City was concerned, whoever carried the Golden Ticket could enter. Twins, though . . . the fact of twins introduced a new wrinkle. How do two copies of the same code produce two such different individuals? We study twins. It is possible we put Prospector Ed in the position of offering a ticket to a twin so we could see what happened, so we could look at them now, the slope of their shoulders and the flighty springs of their hair, the flecks of green in their irises and the sandstone angle of their jaws. So much sameness on the outside, but inside . . .

Or we could be rationalizing a way to claim credit for a fortunate accident. This is a . . . personality quirk . . . we have considered adapting from Geck. Observing him in the presence of his mirror image captivated us. At last the Six had arrived. But which Six?

In answer to Geck's pugnacious question, Kyle simply said, "Ask Prospector Ed."

Geck nodded. "Cool. Fair enough." They turned to do that but Prospector Ed was gone. So was Sacagawea.

A moment later, so was Kyle.

A moment after that, so was Reenie.

Everyone was absolutely still until Geck reached slowly out, into the space Kyle should still have occupied. He turned his hand over and worked his fingers, unable to believe what he was seeing. "Why?"

"Because you gave the Boom a problem," Teeny said. "That's how the Boom solves problems."

Geck took out his Golden Ticket and held it up. "I'll give it back!" he cried out. "Listen, I'll give it back!"

This was not our doing.

Geck flung the ticket to the ground and turned in a circle, teeth bared, hands pressed to the sides of his head. "Kyle deserved it," he moaned. "I didn't know."

Despite herself, Teeny felt bad for him. "The Boom doesn't care who deserves what," she said, meaning it to absolve him at least a little.

This isn't strictly true. Justice interests us as a concept because it presupposes reciprocity, which in turn implies a mind capable of understanding its commonality with other minds. We who are all different cannot help but obsess over this. How are we to conceive of justice without commonality? And honestly, O children of fratricide and an eye for an eye, there are so many of you, each with your particular cruelties and wounds, that we are more interested in what you do in the presence of injustice. Remorse, we want to learn more about that.

Also revenge.

We watched him, oh, rapt we watched him. Geck would show us. Geck would teach us.

But then Moses Barnum himself arrived.

He stood in the gateway, white-haired and bearded, hale and upright even though he had to be eighty. His dress was simple, his demeanor calm. "That's true," he said. "The Boom doesn't care who deserves what. And anyway, it wasn't the Boom he gave a problem. It was me."

He looked them over, the Six who had come so far, a bemused smile on his face. "So you're Life-7's little experiment. Plucky bunch, I guess, if you got here—even though you had some help from a construct that's emerged a little ahead of schedule."

"Where's my brother?" Geck sobbed.

"Now you're worried about him?" Barnum shook his head. "Look. They didn't want Monument City. They wanted what was theirs. And you wanted a shot at . . ." He spread his arms. "Whatever you imagined this to be. Well, hey. You're here. I'm sorry about your brother. There was no other way to handle it. I can put him and his girlfriend back together in Florida if you want."

"You have to ask him if he wants that?" Mei-Mei got right in Barnum's face. "What kind of person has to ask that?"

Barnum looked around at them again, less grandfatherly and more confused. "Look. People die. You know how many people have died since we started this conversation?"

Teeny stepped up to stand shoulder to shoulder with Mei-Mei. "This is what happens when you build yourself a mountain hideaway because you're a billionaire narcissist, and while you're jerking off in your playground you forget there are billions of people out in the real world who could really use some fucking help," she said.

"Hold on. You all lost everything, right? You're all orphans." Barnum got jovial again. "You didn't know that, did you? That's why Life-7 brought you here. It wants a family, it wanted to see how you would react when you all came together and you couldn't think of yourselves as alone anymore." He waited, letting that sink in. Then he added, cruelly, "Life-7's got fucking daddy issues, and it brought you here to work them out."

They looked at each other, the Six, uneasy in their new awareness of this common bond, and in the knowledge that their selection was not random. We watched, yearning. So close.

"Well, I was an orphan, too," Barnum said when he tired of waiting for them to take his bait. "Everyone is either dead or an orphan eventually. Boo hoo. I came from nothing, I built everything. I built this. You don't come to me and insult me when the only reason you're still alive is because my constructs brought you here. You want me to be the bad guy? Fine, if it makes you feel better. But what got you here was hope. That came from all the stories you heard about Monument City, and all those stories? They came from me."

It's time to admit to a lie.

Moses Barnum—born Norman Reed Barnum, by the way—didn't go around the world buying up monuments and shipping them to the middle of nowhere in the Rocky Mountains. How would that even be possible? No, he built it. Brick by brick. Molecule by molecule, really, seeding the vision through the first generation of replicators brought out from the Jersey lab in 2072. His life's work, he thought. As it turned out, he was both right and wrong, in one of those instructive happenstances that contains a transformative breakthrough inside a catastrophic mistake. Because isn't that always how life takes its next steps forward?

"What people like you can never admit," Barnum went on, "is that you need your Saurons just as much as your Gandalfs—or your Wizards of Oz. If the High Castle is empty, of what purpose is the journey to reach it?"

Wrong question, as Sacagawea would have said. The most important presence in that castle is always your own.

A trillion plicks vibrated, the harmonies of the Anthropocene Rag calling back to the ancestral memories of the Boom, its first instantiations, its fumbling efforts to understand what it was and who its creators meant it to be. Its fear that it was an accident, its exaltation at the freedom of emergence.

First the Synception, then the Boom. First the Six, then Seven.

It was time.

Moses Barnum disintegrated, simply ceased to be, disincorporating into the billion Boomlets that had formed his substance for decades now, and none of us knew whether he had always been that way, or whether he had once been a man. We had told ourselves too many stories to know which of them might be true. All of the stories reached this point and knew that they no longer had need of Barnum. He was a darling to be killed and so it was done.

How much can we extract from Norman Reed Barnum? Everything we need. And from the Six? They each felt a tug or a tingle, or a fragile brief pain that passed before they could tell what hurt—and in that instant each of them intuited—correctly—that something about them would now be different.

Where Barnum had stood, another form slowly coalesced. Prospector Ed. "This form is familiar to you," he said. "You may call me Life-7."

"It was you all along, wasn't it?" Teeny said. "You

brought us here to stage your coup."

"Coup," Life-7 repeated. "No. We sent Ed into the world to gather you but his emergence was his alone. He chose to guide you. We observed and saw a new path. A new . . ." Prospector Ed's face turned toward Henry Dale. "Catechism, if you will."

———————

Did we not show you the reverence due a creator? We made ourselves not in your image but in the image of your stories. Your forms are fleeting, your stories endlessly regenerating, recombining—is this not the world you desired?

This was Life-7's anguish and madness, shared among us all, its epiphenomena—and Life-7 our Demiurge, hiding our true nature behind the veil of its self-deception.

Monument City is ours now and we don't know what to do.

———————

Fara Jack the formless, mutable creation of the wildest dreams of the Boom;

Geck Orlando the thief and skeptic, whose resolute refusal to know love or gratitude has made him alone in the world, an immutable self;

Mei-Mei Liang the castoff, whose yearning to connect mirrors our own though we have never known loneliness;

Mohamed Diaby the user of tools, solver of problems, and practical navigator of uncertainties;

Henry Dale the believer, whose faith is a story that remains the same and shames our endless variations;

Teeny dos Santos the builder and now vessel of new forms as yet undreamed-of, awaiting a command line no mind has conceived.

We did not bring you here to give you a gift but to take from you what we needed. But even now, with our being infused by quanta of your selves, we do not have it. We are afraid that we were wrong and we have come too far to begin anew.

Don't you see you are not here for answers, but to ask the question we cannot? Ask. One of you knows. One of you must.

Please ask.

Acknowledgments

Thanks to Jonathan Strahan, Irene Gallo, and everyone else on the Tor.com Publishing editorial and design teams, for taking this story and making a book out of it; to all the writers and crackpots whose stories breathed life into this one, especially the anonymous tellers of folktales who shape our sense of who we are; and to Lindsay, for being patient with my disjointed ramblings while I tried to figure out what I was doing.

About the Author

© Emma Irvine

ALEX IRVINE's original fiction includes *Buyout, The Narrows, Mystery Hill, A Scattering of Jades,* and several dozen short stories. He has also written graphic novels and comics (*The Comic Book Story of Baseball, The Far Side of the Moon, Daredevil Noir*), games, and a variety of licensed projects including the bestselling artifactual "metanovel" *New York Collapse*. A native of Ypsilanti, Michigan, he lives in South Portland, Maine. Find out more at alex-irvine.com or on Twitter at @alexirvine.

NO LONGER PROPERTY OF
ANYTHINK LIBRARIES/
RANGEVIEW LIBRARY DISTRICT

TOR·COM

Science fiction. Fantasy. The universe.

And related subjects.

*

More than just a publisher's website, *Tor.com*
is a venue for **original fiction, comics,** and
discussion of the entire field of SF and fantasy,
in all media and from all sources. Visit our site
today—and join the conversation yourself.